The Blue Bu
©Graham Singleton Reed.

First Edition 2013
Edited by Graham and Jean Hulley
ISBN: 978-1-291-64128-8

To my parents:

Walter John Reed
and
Faith Marguerite Fisher

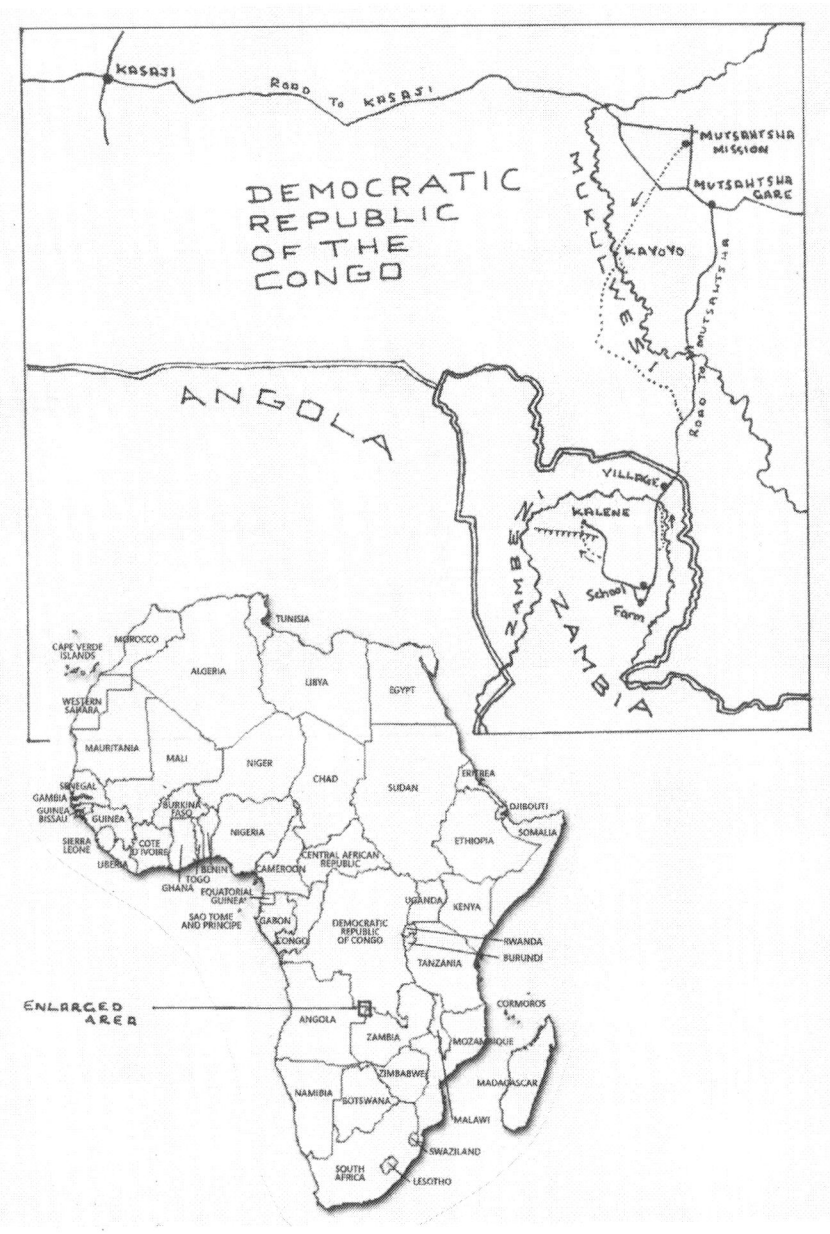

Foreword

On the 13th of February 1959 a little boy was born at Kasaji Mission, arriving a few minutes before midnight, and thus avoiding being a Valentine's Baby. He was the fourth child born to Walter John Reed and Faith Marguerite Reed. His parents were undecided what to call him. They had a deep admiration for the great twentieth century evangelist, Dr Billy Graham, and wanted to name their new baby after him, but neither parent liked the name Billy, so they decided to call him Graham Singleton. His second name being that of his maternal grandfather.

This book is a novel, and as such, it is a work of fiction. However much of what unfolds in its pages describes things and places that really did happen in the mid-1960s in what was then the Province of Katanga in the Democratic Republic of the Congo (not to be mistaken with another country to the north-west, confusingly called Congo).

It will not take much detective work on the part of the reader to discover that the main character, Billy is modeled on the author as a boy. It will not take long for the reader to work out that he loved life in Africa but hated going to boarding school from the tender age of six. Some of the events he describes there did actually happen, but the greater part of the book, including all of its latter parts is fictional.

It is only as the author has grown older that he has come to appreciate the great sacrifice that many of the teachers at the school had to make to be there, and to provide him with an education; An education which stood him in good stead when he moved to England as a twelve year old.

Descriptions of mercenary activity in that part of Africa are, sadly, taken from real accounts. Mike Hoare and 5 Commando really did exist. He had about 1000 men at his command, but what happens to them in the pages of this book, whilst being informed by real events, is also fictional. Appendix 2 gives a real account from the time.

The map on the following page is roughly accurate, and some of the places can be seen on Google Earth, particularly those places with airstrips, all of which still exist.

As you read this please take a moment to reflect that in many parts of the DRC today, conflict continues, with many thousands of families affected. If you believe in the power of prayer, keep this vast country and its people in your prayers too.

Chapter 1

The curtains fly open theatrically. The sunrise, golden and warm, falls on Billy's face, welcoming and bright. His hair is yellow He is full of life. His eyes are a vivid blue. The dry season is just beginning and the world is still full of the life left behind by six months of rain. Giant land-snails take advantage of the last few minutes of dewy moisture, sliding purposefully towards cascades of petunias tumbling out of a flower trough running around the edge of the veranda.

Billy scoops up his butterfly net and runs outside in his pyjamas, lured by a flash of colour dancing around the fading petals of a moon-flower that climbs vigorously up a pillar just outside his room. Billy knows this is not one he has in his already extensive collection of butterflies. This is new treasure. His heart beats fast. His quarry has landed on a creamy bloom, wings quivering, and proboscis deep in the sweet scented heart of the flower. He creeps forward slowly, net poised. A little closer, and then a little more, and then he sweeps the net down as quickly as he can, catching the whole flower and knocking it to the ground. He is surprised to find that the creature he has caught is not a butterfly at all. It's robust body and powerful wings give the impression of being a small hummingbird. Billy presses the net down, trapping it against the floor. Now he can see that it is a moth, its wings exquisitely marked with microscopic patterns in greys and browns, and its stout body circled with stripes of black and bright pink. Still trapped by the net, Billy pushes his thumb down firmly on its head, and it stops moving.

Billy is aware of his mother's voice calling him for breakfast.

"Mummy, Look what I've caught! I think it's another hawk moth". Carefully he empties it out onto the wooden table. His mother helps him to pin it into a display box, already half full. This is one of his favourites, and at the centre is a magnificent death's-head hawk moth. Billy's new acquisition is pinned proudly next to it.

Faith is tall and slender with rich chocolate coloured hair pulled back purposefully and soft brown eyes behind her glasses. She moves quickly and lightly around her large rudimentary kitchen carrying a plastic jug, the contents of which she is whisking vigorously. She takes a saucepan of porridge from the wood stove. Billy is holding a bowl ready as Charlie runs in to get his share.

King George is stoking up the fire in the stove. He is profoundly deaf, and so he is unable to speak Lunda, English or French. Far from being a handicap his own flamboyant sign language overcomes all communication barriers, and the loud vocal noises he uses, makes it impossible for anyone to be unaware that he is in the house! He carries his rather presumptuous title with great pride. Being named after a British monarch is considered a great honour in his family, and he is not short of self-confidence. Faith and John Walker have employed him to work around the house and to look after Billy and Charlie whilst they are at work. The boys adore him, regularly dragging him off to get involved in their adventures, until he waves his hands wildly, emitting loud screeches to show that he feels they are going too far!

He is still a little bit outraged after yesterday's caper! Charlie, aged six had already lit a fire under a big old tree whilst Billy was catching grasshoppers with his butterfly net. Once caught, they were thrown into the fire to roast, and then removed with a stick and eaten. Several different kinds of grasshopper had already been sampled before King George was summoned and offered one. He displayed his horror with wild gesticulations, and very convincingly mimed being sick. Crisis over, he beckoned the boys to follow him to a bare patch of earth under another tree. Crouching in the dust with a small twig he began digging and soon turned up a moth pupa, wriggling inside its temporary armour. King George held it up triumphantly. A few more minutes and there were a dozen or more in his palm. Taking Charlie firmly by the hand he led the boys back to the fire and carefully laid the chrysalises side by side on a broad stick. Gently, he placed the stick on the edge of the fire in exactly the right place to roast them without blackening them. Then he held one up and dropped it into his mouth, crunching it satisfyingly. Billy and Charlie couldn't wait to try them. Their leathery skins gave way to a juicy centre. King George showed them how to spit out the skin once they had been thoroughly chewed.

Billy and Charlie like the fact that King George isn't in a position to make detailed reports back to Mama Faith, and the boys are selective about what they tell their parents at the end of the day!

Now they sit at the dining room table and wait for Dad to come in and say grace before ladling wild African honey with real dead bees onto their porridge. Billy leans his butterfly net against the table. John has already had his breakfast but comes in to open the big old family Bible and to read the recommended verses for the day. Then he takes out his copy of "Echoes of Service" and finds the missionaries included on the prayer list for the 28th May 1967. The names are familiar, but where is Uttar Pradesh? It sounds so far away, so exotic! With bowed heads and clasped hands each person prays, but by the time it is Billy's turn, his mind is in the far reaches of the garden wondering if there are any more baby chameleons on the poinsettia tree. A gentle dig in the ribs from his mother brings him back to prayers.

At the last "Amen", Faith throws off her apron, kisses her husband and hurries to jump on a dilapidated bicycle. Billy knows that his mum is going to the hospital where she works. She is trained as a midwife and a tropical diseases nurse. Billy likes it best when she gets home and the sun is setting. For a few minutes she is too tired to move and collapses onto the old wicker settee waiting for King George to emerge loudly with a steaming cup of tea. This is when she is at her most huggable, so he will throw his arms all the way round his mummy and snuggle into a long hug. Sometimes Charlie will snuggle up on the other side, and sometimes, Whiskers the putty-nosed guenon, the family's small but very pugnacious monkey will try and muscle in on the act jealously. Snowy the cat ignores this mass demonstration of affection. With her back to everyone she flicks her tail disdainfully.

But for now, the morning is young and full of promise. Billy asks to get down and rushes to dress and then clean his teeth before charging out into the garden. He has his rounds to do. Old Nyatchinyuma is sweeping the path with her twig broom.

First stop, the poinsettia tree. Two days ago he had found three tiny chameleons, no bigger than his little finger and perfectly formed. They are now living in an empty fish tank and are being regularly supplied with dead flies. Billy looks carefully but can find no more.

Next stop the flower bed beside the main path up to the house. This is one of Billy's favourite places. Although he is only eight he knows all the plants in that bed as if they are his personal friends. He has been watching a zinnia plant that has come up later than the rest, every day wondering what colour it will be. To his delight it is open! An amazing fuchsia pink, and there at its centre is a tiny praying mantis, about half an inch long, sitting up with its front feet together prayerfully waiting for an insect to visit the new flower. It is exactly the same vibrant pink as the bloom, with tiny sparkling eyes like jewels set into its head. This is too much for Billy. He sprints inside, catches King George by the arm and drags him, protesting all the way, to look at what he has found. King George is more interested in the culinary merits of the insect world than he is of its beauty, and Billy soon moves on to inspect Lucy in her coop.

Lucy is a small and rather scruffy looking bantam hen. Billy's dad has put her into the incubating crate with six table tennis balls to see if she will earn the right to sit on some proper eggs. She is situated against the house at a point right under the chimney. Fluffed up, and sitting firmly on her fake clutch, she eyes Billy with as haughty an expression as a small bantam can muster. Billy thinks she has earned the right to look a bit proud of herself. The wet season went out with a bang last week when a huge bolt of lightning coursed down the chimney sending rubble crashing into the sitting room just as Billy and Charlie were listening to their dad try to read a bedtime story over the deafening sound of a tropical downpour hammering on the corrugated iron roof. Some of the rubble crashed down on to poor Lucy's coop, and everyone was sure that daylight would reveal a squashed chicken. Miraculously, although the rubble was piled up all round her coop, Lucy was unharmed and still sitting tight on her half dozen table tennis balls!

"Today's the day," says Billy seriously. "Daddy's going to give you some real eggs." Lucy blinks, but her expression does not change.

Billy and Charlie have been banned from going around the back of the house on health and safety grounds, ever since the incident with Charlie and the 44 gallon drum sunken into the ground behind the bathroom. In the dry season all the bath water drains into it, and when it is half full, King George fills it up with cow manure and chicken droppings and then uses it as liquid fertilizer on the roses. Unfortunately Charlie had fallen head first into this potent mixture and would have drowned if King George had not seen two little feet sticking out one morning. He was hauled out and hosed down, but the smell stayed with him and filled the house for at least a week.

Almost next to the forbidden drum is the place where the hot water drum sits, above an open fire. Every Friday it is lit early in the morning to provide hot water later in the day. It's not the bath that Billy looks forward to so much as the sweet potatoes that are thrown into the fire and come out ready to eat at lunch time on Fridays. King George will juggle them onto a rock where they will be cut open, liberally spread with Stork Margarine and then blissfully eaten. Billy can think of nothing more delicious. He has learned to tell the time like his African friends, just by looking at the sun. He creeps round to the back of the house to check that the fire is burning and the sweet potatoes are baking, but finds that King George's morning is not going well.

Billy is trying to understand why he is so upset. Waving his arms up and down, he is pointing to the small bungalow built onto the side of the house. This is where Billy's Granny lives with a little corridor leading into the house. She has all the facilities to live an independent life but comes into the house to share supper with the rest of the family each evening. She is not quite as deaf as King George, but she needs two hearing-aids to tune into the world. She spends a lot of her time writing or painting.

When Billy arrives at King George's side he can see Rhonda has arrived with Granny's breakfast on a tray; a grapefruit cut in half, smothered in sugar and a cup of tea on a saucer. Granny usually leaves her door unlocked, but she has got annoyed with Rhonda who does not understand about knocking and always walks in with breakfast just as Granny is in a state of undress. Now she has decided the only thing to do is to lock the door. This has created a problem for everyone. Any amount of banging on windows and doors is not catching Granny's attention, and King George can see through a crack in the curtains, that she is still lying on her bed. Through wild and very excited gestures he is now trying to explain to Ronda, Billy and Charlie, who has arrived to find out what the commotion is about, that he believes Granny is dead! Ronda drops the tray in shock and runs away, whilst King George hunts around for a very long bamboo cane.

There is a hole, low down in the wall of Granny's bedroom where a brick has been removed to provide ventilation. The bamboo is carefully passed through the hole towards Granny's feet, sticking out from under her sheet. King George maneuvers it with great concentration, his eyes focused, his tongue out, and all the time making loud and urgent noises. Suddenly the bamboo finds its target and granny explodes into action, jumping out of her bed as if she is being attacked by a snake! She picks up a slipper and begins to beat the sheet incase there is anything dangerous underneath it, whilst everyone outside waves frantically, hoping she will see the commotion through the little gap in her curtains.

Daddy says Granny is a "character".

Chapter 2

The sun is getting hot now, and Billy's next stop on his tour of inspection is the underneath of the mango tree half way down the road to the hospital. There are three good reasons to go there. First it is about the coolest place on the mission station. The mango leaves make a thick, dark shade. Secondly most days see ripe mangoes falling from the tree, and Billy loves mangoes. Lastly, this is a really good place for catching butterflies, especially in the heat of the day, when rotting mangoes are at their smelliest, and the butterflies, hungry for fermenting fruit, are most active. Billy sits, net in hand, with his back against the tree and sighs with pure happiness. There is only one thing right at the back of his young mind that worries him, and that is the dreaded thought of going back to school, but it is weeks, before that happens, and for the moment, life is perfect.

Billy jumps as Whiskers leaps onto his shoulder from behind, dragging a disemboweled mango up with him.

"Oh, it's only you!"

The little monkey happily buries his face into the half rotted fruit, and emerges covered in the orange-yellow flesh. Billy picks up a fresh mango leaf and carefully strips it half-way along the central vein. And then strips half the opposite side to make a propeller shape. He picks up a thin twig and pushes it through the middle and then blows on it to make it spin.

From where he is sitting Billy can see the house, only a few hundred yards away. The veranda is busy with people running around in obvious preparation for some kind of expedition. At the centre of the commotion is Granny, wearing a nightie which has been liberally splashed with paint. Two small African boys, and Rhonda (who has apparently recovered from her fright) are fetching all manner of equipment. A stool, an easel, paper, pieces of hardboard, linseed oil, white spirit, brushes, water pots, a very large hat and a walking stick. King George is convinced that only he is qualified to organise everybody, so he is running around making loud noises and waving at everyone, even though he has no idea what Granny is asking for. After some considerable time the party sets off down the grand avenue from the house, through a spectacular arch of Golden Shower and on down the middle of the road. Fortunately cars only appear about once a month, so there is little prospect of Granny and her entourage getting run over. Every ten yards or so the whole party has to stop and turn to face the house, so that Granny can assess whether she has reached the right spot to start painting. Eventually she decides that the house will look best, when viewed from under the branches of the mango tree, so she sets up her studio in the middle of the main road, next to the tree. Billy gets up and carefully tip-toes through the Christ-thorn hedge that borders both sides of the road to get to his granny. Granny is not a natural receiver of hugs. She holds her arms up as if to keep them out of the way.

"Don't hug me Billy, I'm covered in paint."

"But it's all dry, Granny!"

"I know dear, but it will soon be wet."

Billy steps back with a puzzled look on his face, whilst Granny fusses about getting everything in the right place and regularly looking at the house through the one clear lens she has in her glasses. Finally everything is ready, and an expectant hush falls on the whole gathering. Granny is holding one brush upright at arms length, measuring the height and breadth of the house, then suddenly she says:

"I really ought to have powdered my nose before coming out, Rhonda dear, take me back to the house."

Billy knows that Granny will never say the word "toilet".

Eventually Granny returns and the first exciting brush strokes add life and colour to a new piece of hardboard that has already been painted white. Billy is always mesmerised by watching his granny paint. It seems like a wonderful kind of magic to see the picture come to life, and he loves the smell of the linseed oil. King George makes the party complete by balancing a bone-china cup of Ceylon tea down the road for Granny to sip between brush strokes, but by this time Billy has gone.

He is sitting up straight on a log, right next to Charlie. They are both munching their Friday sweet potato. This is a moment too precious for talking, so apart from loud chomping (it is bad manners to eat with your mouth closed), silence prevails.

Billy's dad appears and picks up his potato from the rock where it is cooling off. He sits down on the log too, but knows better than to start talking before the eating is finished.

Chapter 3

"Come on boys, time for rest hour."

Mum is arriving on her bike as the family move back into the shade of the house. Mum and Dad both work very long days and by noon this part of the Katanga province of the DRC is very hot, despite being some five thousand feet above sea level. Rest hour is non-negotiable in the Walker house. Mum and Dad sleep, whilst Charlie is allowed to play with his Lego. Billy loves to read anything written by Gerald Durrell. His stories of animal-collecting around the world capture his imagination, and almost create an extension of his own life. He lies on his bed, propped up on his elbows whilst Snowy the cat tries hard to steal his attention, and fails. His now dog-eared copy of the Baffut Beagles transports him out of the bush he knows so well to the mysterious world of the Cameroon Rain Forest. He hardly notices his mother's voice as she announces the end of rest hour and blows him a kiss before pedaling off to the hospital again. In moments Charlie appears like a caged animal, set free. He has a large glass jar and a fishing net. He is determined to get Billy to join him on a fishing expedition to the Kalemba river, only about a mile away. Billy throws his book on the bed, picks up his butterfly net and rushes out of the house.

"Hey! Wait for me!" shouts Charlie, "You'll make me wheeze!"

But Billy is already running back along the dusty road, past Granny's temporarily deserted easel to the point where he turns left opposite the hospital. Hands on his knees he waits to get his breath and to let Charlie catch up, then they skip down to the river. On the way they are joined by Billy's friend Rubeni. The bush gives way to boggy plain, and Billy is distracted by tall steeple flowers growing amongst head high grass.

Charlie is already knee deep in the little river, peering intensely through crystal clear water for any sign of fish camouflaged against the stony bed. It's easy to tell when Charlie is concentrating; he sticks his tongue out and bites it whilst his brow becomes furrowed. His shorts always look too big for him, pulled up high around his waist. He lowers his net very slowly into the water with one hand held up indicating to Billy and Rubeni not to come any closer. He edges his net a millimetre at a time up stream for a whole minute then with a lightning fast swish he swoops the net forwards and upwards. There in the bottom of the net is a tiny fish glinting like polished silver with bright red fins. Charlie empties it into his jar, where it looks twice its actual size. He fetches some bright green weed which he stuffs into his jar to make a happier home for his captive.

Satisfied for the moment, he passes his net to Rubeni who paddles lightly across the river. Here the current has undercut the bank, and it is a little deeper. Rubeni gently angles the net under the bank and trawls against the current in one long movement. His efforts are rewarded by not one but two minute mudfish; tiny jet black catfish about the size and shape of tadpoles except for their whiskers. They are tipped in to Charlie's jar where they wriggle lazily to the bottom. Billy is using his butterfly net, which is a little larger than the fishing net. It has a flat front edge which he is holding firmly on the bed of the quickest part of the river. It is shallow and rocky here. He shuffles his net up to a point just below a large flat rock, and then reaches down into the water to lift the rock from the side facing the net. At the same time he scoops the net under the rock and up. Billy has caught a sucker fish. It is mottled with browns and ochre, and has a sucker under its head that it uses to hold on to rocks in the swift current. Billy is quick to point out that his inch and a half long capture is the largest of the day!

The boys put the jar on the grass and then lie in a three pointed star around it to observe their miniature exotic fish tank, and then roll over onto their backs to watch cumulus clouds against a vivid cerulean sky.

The sun is sinking, the day is cooling, and in the distance there is the unmistakable sound of the gong. John and Faith know that the boys are completely safe on the mission station, so they are allowed to wander wherever they want, but they know that it is time for food or bed when the gong goes. All three boys jump up, the fish are returned to their original home, and the race is on to get back to the house.

Rubeni loves eating with his friends, he can't understand why they feel the need to use what look like metal implements of torture to get the food from the plate to the mouth, but he loves trying all the strange things they eat; like baked beans on toast! He also loves it when Billy and Charlie are allowed to come and eat with his family. They are even learning a few eating manners at last!

By the time Rubeni slips away into the moonlight and heads home, Billy's dad is ready to walk up to the generator house where the oily old monster is waiting to be cranked into action. Dad reminds Billy to put his wellies on. "You don't want to step on a snake without them." He reminds Billy. The generator inevitably seems grumpy and bad tempered. It always refuses to start with the first vigorous turn of the crank handle, and dad always seems to have to talk to it and adjust it before it eventually splutters into action. As it does so the lights slowly come up in the house and hospital.

Billy is excited! Dad has been to Mutshutsha Gare to pick up the post, and a package has arrived from England. It is from Billy's older brother and sister, and it contains a "Noggin the Nog" record. Once back in the house the gramophone is dusted off and the record is placed carefully on the turntable. It is the first time the boys have seen a 45rpm record. The only other records stacked in the corner are Dad's classical collection, including Handel's Messiah, which he likes to put on after church on Sundays. He switches the speed from 33 to 45 and everyone sits on the settee ready to listen. A strange and wonderful story emerges about Noggin the kindly Viking king and an amazing Ice Dragon. Billy imagines a world covered in ice! All too soon the record finishes and the needle clicks each time the record goes round. Billy and Charlie race to be fist into bed.

Mum comes in to give the boys a hug and to sing them the bedtime song she sings every night. She kneels between the two beds and holds hands with Charlie and Billy. Her voice is clear and sweet:

> "Jesus, tender Shepherd, hear me;
> Bless Thy little lambs tonight;
> Through the darkness be Thou near them;
> Watch their sleep till morning light.
>
> All this day thy hand has led us,
> And we thank Thee for Thy care;
> Thou hast clothed us, warmed and fed us,
> Listen to our evening prayer.
>
> Let our sins be all forgiven;
> Bless the friends we love so well;
> Take us, when we die, to Heaven,
> Happy there with Thee to dwell.
> Amen.
>
> *(Mary Lundie Duncan)*

Charlie is asleep before the third verse and doesn't feel his mother's kiss, or the fingers that run lovingly through his mop of brown hair. Billy gives his mum a kiss and then lies in the darkness and allows his imagination to explore the icy world of Noggin the Nog. Imagining drifts into dreaming.

Chapter 4

Far, far away, a thousand kilometres across the bush, in the same country but in a different world, there is trouble. Anger against a government heavily controlled by Europeans has spawned a rebellion.

The spiritmen from a huge part of Eastern Congo have come together to retake control of their land. They are known as the "Simbas", the Swahili word for "lions". The Congolese army are terrified of them. They believe that the Simbas are immune to bullets, so town after town falls, as soldiers flee in panic, often without firing a shot. The spiritmen do terrible things to those they see as supporting the government, including teachers and government workers.

There is no line to show the border between Angola, Zambia, and the Congo. Mike Hoare has quickly renamed his troupe of Mercenaries the "5 Commando". On the shoulder of their camouflage is a badge showing a blue goose in flight. Their bank accounts have already received a heavy deposit of cash, and there will be another payment if they complete their mission successfully. This is not Hoare's first incursion into this part of the Congo. For three brief years, the province of Katanga had declared itself independent from the rest of the country under President Moise Tshombe. Mike Hoare has become a name synonymous with terror, whispered by villagers and separatists, who remembered his ruthless campaign of death and destruction in the name of a united Congolese Republic. Meet him on the street or in a bar, and you would be struck by his cheerful, polite manner- the kind of person that makes you feel good. But meet him on the other side of a rifle, and you will find nothing but cold, calculated brutality.

Two Landrovers move through the darkness, bumping over rocks on a little used track through the bush. Inside are five South African mercenaries. 5 Commando, weapons slung around their shoulders and faces smeared with camouflage, peer forward into the dark. Their instructions are clear, and there is no prospect of any resistance. They do not even know the name of the village sleeping half a mile ahead of them. Headlights off, engines off, and the men slip out of their vehicles without speaking. Hoare waves them forward and they run to within yards of the circle of huts.

It is silent except for the lazy barking of a dog.

Then pandemonium breaks loose. Machine gun fire at waist height peppers holes through the flimsy huts, ricocheting from corrugated iron roofs and walls. For a few minutes there are screams and in the dark, the silhouettes of figures stumbling out of their homes, but they do not get far. An orange glow springs up as the first hut is set on fire, illuminating a few villagers that are running towards the bush. The light makes them easy targets. Even the dog has stopped barking. In nine short minutes thirty six men, women and children are dead or dying.

The mercenaries know that they are still hundreds of miles from their destination, but they plan to generate a tide of terror that will make them feared more than the spiritmen, long before they arrive in Stanleyville, even if many innocent people have to die.

Each man has been told; "Leave no one alive".

Chapter 5

That little cloud is taking shape in Billy's perfect world, the one called school. Every day it gets a tiny bit bigger. He tries to push it to the back of his mind, but it is always there. At least Charlie will be joining him this term. Now there is only a week to go. Billy lies in bed worrying about it, finding it hard to sleep, but wanting to put a brave face on it.

He remembers how it was the first time. The strange smell of the boy's dormitory. A big warehouse of a room. No cupboards or wardrobes. Everything that Billy owned had to stay in a battered suitcase on a chair by his bed. No privacy. Iron roof. His bed and how badly he missed his mum and dad. A hard world to adapt to when you are six years old.

Billy's little heart was broken. He learned quickly not to show any tears for fear of being bullied, but inside he cried and cried for weeks. He couldn't eat, and felt so homesick that he told the matron "I need to go to the maternity". Secretly he thought he might find his mum there, but she was far away in another country, There was no one to hug, no one to understand how abandoned he felt. No one to talk to, just a big gaping hole.

In lessons he gazed out of the windows and thought about home, about King George, about his pets and his precious mum and dad. Billy was afraid of most of the teachers. It felt like they were looking for ways of punishing him all the time, so he learned to do as he was told and to try and keep out of trouble.

There are only two terms a year, and each is eighteen weeks long. Billy feels like each term is a life sentence.

Now Billy is about to start grade three, but he dreads going back. Slowly he stops being the carefree boy and a weight settles on his little shoulders. It begins to take the wind out of his sails.

Mum and Dad are trying to sell the idea of boarding school to Charlie. Everyday they tell him more about all the wonderful things that will happen, but Billy stays quiet. He knows that his mum was once a pupil there in the days when travelling long distances meant being carried in a hammock strung between two poles by four strong Africans. Billy can see the sadness in her eyes when she talks about school. He wonders if she remembers what it was really like.

The tactics seem to be working, as Charlie is excited about going to school. There is just one hurdle that needs to be overcome before Charlie can start. He has suffered from some bad bouts of asthma, and the school wants him to have a proper chest x-ray before he can be allowed to start. The nearest x-ray machine is eighty miles away at Kasaji, a bigger mission station with a better equipped hospital and a doctor. Now he has an adventure to look forward to before the dreaded day, something he can focus on instead of school.

Chapter 6

Dad bows his head. His strong hand makes Billy feel safe.

"Heavenly Father, thank you for all your provision for us as a family. Please keep us safe on our journey today. Surround us with your protection. In Jesus' name we ask it. Amen."

Everything is packed in the boot of the old Ford Zephyr. Dad has topped up the oil and he has used up half the jerry can of petrol making sure there is more than enough fuel to complete the journey. The spare tyre is checked, along with Dad's tool box, a shovel and a rope. Instructions are left with King George for looking after the house and keeping an eye on Granny. He will sleep in the visitor's room. King of the house!

Eighty miles in a low slung saloon car along a rarely used dirt track demands a lot of concentration, and a small squadron of guardian angels! The shock absorbers are tested to the limit. The sump gets scraped and bashed by the occasional large rock. There is mud to get stuck in during the wet season, when most people avoid driving altogether, and there is sand to get stuck in during the dry season. There are always parts of the road that are totally unusable either because the road has got washed away, or because something has been abandoned in the middle of it. In the former case the shovel comes out, branches are cut down and the road is made good enough to drive across. Dad prefers to get all his passengers out to walk alongside the car on these tricky parts of the road. In the latter case, there is usually no choice other than to drive around the obstacle by maneuvering the car through the bush. This might mean cutting down small trees and leveling minor anthills before progress can be made. The eighty mile journey to Kasaji often takes the whole day with a rest hour break by a stream.

Billy loves the break most of all. There is a large flat rock sloping down to a small river just beyond the village of Mungolunga. Driving through a village promotes you to the status of celebrity! On hearing an approaching vehicle, everyone comes out to see who it is. The road is lined with smiling faces, waving hands and running children. Lunch and rest hour would be impossible in a village, but this place is always quiet except for the grasshoppers, "etu" birds and the inescapable call of the "work-harder" pigeon, so named, because of its insistent and persistent cry that sounds so much like "work harder". The "etu" is a thick strip of forest that grows alongside streams and rivers where the trees can draw on water all year round. It is often only a few yards wide.

Billy doesn't really notice the birds, he is excited to be in a new place for catching butterflies. First he makes a careful inspection of the radiator grill. He knows that the car is working hard to catch butterflies for him, but most of them end up too tatty for his collection. Today however he carefully untangles a magnificent specimen of *Precis cebrene*. Its wings coloured with sunset yellow and ginger splashes, surrounded by jagged black shapes, and on the lower wings, hiding away, are two vivid, "eyes". His dad fetches the butterfly jar from the boot of the car.

The picnic rock slopes from a place in the open bush where it is too hot to sit, down into the deep shade beside the river. It runs out just before the water. Here there is a miniature sandy beach where small animals come to drink.

In the middle of the day the damp fringe of the beach is a colourful quivering mass of butterflies, each with its proboscis sucking up moisture. Billy creeps down the rock to a spot where he can closely observe without frightening them into a cloud of fluttering wings. At first he can see that there is nothing new, so he just enjoys the spectacle of literally hundreds of insects, happily flitting in and out. He loves the way they quiver as they feed, as if from pure ecstasy!

Then his heart nearly stops. He freezes. His net is in his hand, but he cannot move it. An unbelievably bright blue butterfly has landed in amongst all the yellows, golds and browns. The under side of its wings are darkly coloured, camouflaged against the leaves and mud, but slowly, responding to a ray of sunlight it opens its wings to reveal bright, iridescent, electric blue wings. Billy gasps. He has never seen anything so exquisite in his whole life. He wants to turn and call his mum, but he is afraid that if he does he will frighten it away. Now the angle of its wings reflects the sun directly into Billy's eyes. It is almost dazzling! He is completely transfixed. He cannot bring himself to catch and kill it. It is as if he is looking at the wings of an angel. He just stares at it.

The blue butterfly is bigger and more robust than all the others. These others looked so beautiful to Billy only seconds ago. Now they look dowdy. After a whole minute there is a final flash of kingfisher blue and it is gone. Billy sits down slowly. He can't believe what he has just seen. He can't believe that his net is still unused.

"Are you alright Billy?" His mother calls down to him, seeing him sitting still for such a long time. He says nothing for a few moments, then runs up to explore the picnic box.

After lunch Billy goes on a flower hunt, making a careful check along the edge of the road where a mixture of open sunlight and a damp ditch often yields good results. Billy is not disappointed. Within minutes he has found a group of lime green gladioli, much smaller and more delicate than the blousy ones his mum has planted in the garden at home. Billy thinks the wild ones are so much more beautiful, and he loves the way they try to hide. This one has tiny dots and dashes painted in brick red against the lime green background. Billy gazes at each open flower, and the promising buds all wrapped up and ready to unfurl. He wonders if he will be the only person in the world to see them, and under his breath he tells God how clever he thinks he is.

There is an image etched on Billy's memory, that he will never lose. He wonders why he couldn't try to catch that blue butterfly.

"Something happened to me. I didn't even want to catch it. Maybe God wanted to protect it. It was too beautiful to kill," he thinks.

Dad has the bonnet up on the Zephyr, and he is pouring a bottle of river water into the steaming radiator.

The road ahead is narrow and the grass is over seven feet high. Bowing over the road from both sides it makes a delicate tunnel. In places the tunnel has partly collapsed making it impossible to see the road ahead. Here the blue sky can be seen through a delicate filigree of grasses. Suddenly out of the grass a bushbuck leaps across the road not ten feet in front of the car making everyone jump. The car comes to a stop on a narrow sandy bit of road. Dad tries to get going again, but the back wheels dig down into the sand without moving the car forward. The car is stuck, but dad knows what to do. Out comes the shovel to move the sand in front of the rear wheels, whilst mum and the boys fetch small twigs and sticks to make a miniature ramp and some grip where the sand has been removed. Slowly the big old car begins to move forward, and they are on their way again. By now the temperature has reached a hundred degrees. The car does not know about air conditioning so the windows are open. A cloud of orange dust follows, apparently determined to overtake. It seems particularly keen to get in through the open windows, where it coats everyone with a fine dirty powder.

Chapter 7

Kasaji introduces itself slowly, as more and more low buildings of mud brick, iron and thatch come into view. It is so much bigger than Mutshatsha. Billy notices little stores and shops he does not see at home. For a treat they stop and buy four bottles of Coke. They are deliciously cold. The bottles are scratched and frosted; veterans of recycling. Mum takes her bottle back to change it, when she notices that there is a dead fly floating in it even before she opens it with dad's penknife.

On the far side of the town the car swings right and drives into the mission station. Billy loves the mauve jacaranda trees, with their delicate leaves and drooping cascades of flowers. They make a magical carpet of mauve petals for several days after they fall. In contrast the African tulip tree has thick dark leaves. The flowers are like little bursts of orange and yellow flames, but Billy likes them most when they are still in bud and they make wonderful natural water pistols. Each velvety bud is about two inches long and is full of water. Laying the bud, carefully aimed on the palm of the hand and then punching it sharply with the other hand squirts a shot of water at the unsuspecting target. Billy has learned not to do this when his mum is around, since although the water is clear, the sap inside the petals is full of a powerful yellow dye, and however careful he is, this dye always manages to find a way onto his clothes.

The car draws up at Uncle Terry's house, in a cloud of dust.

Billy's mum points at a house across the compound "That's the house where you were born."

"I know mum. You always tell me that when we come here."

Charlie has already run into the house and is being greeted by Barbara, his favourite aunt. He gets a hug, despite being covered in a layer of dust.

"Hello aunty Bra-bra", he says, almost rugby tackling her.

"There is hot water if you want a bath", smiles Aunty Barbara, as she comes out to greet the family with a tray of lemonade.

The whole family works its way through the bath, just adding a little more water each time some one gets out. The sun is setting through the trees over the hospital, as supper is served, Dr and Mrs Mote arrive to join the meal, but the doctor has some frustrating news. The x-ray machine is not working, and a part has been ordered from Lubumbashi.

It is not expected to arrive until tomorrow, when Mr. Brown is flying in with his Cessna 180. The Walkers will be staying at Kasaji a little longer than they had planned.

Billy lies in his bed putting the day in order so that he can file it away in the back of his mind. He loves travelling even with the heat and dust. He can still vividly see the flash of electric blue from the butterfly he let go. That moment was the highlight of his day. Somehow it feels good to be at Kasaji for a few days. It's a few days before school, and he wonders if it is too much to ask God for the x-ray machine to stay broken for ever.

His mum sings her familiar lullaby.

Chapter 8

Breakfast is nearly over. Uncle Terry has gone up to oversee the making of some new bricks. Mud, clay and straw are mixed with water and then poured into moulds to dry in the sun . There is real milk with the porridge, a treat. Billy is used to drinking powdered milk. After prayers the grown-ups keep talking, as only grown-ups can. Billy has noticed a distant drone. He knows what it is, and so does Charlie.

He is out of the house before he remembers to call over his shoulder: "Please may I get down?"

"Don't get wheezy," his mum calls after him.

He is out of range, and doesn't hear. Billy makes a slight detour to call on his old friend Jonnie. He is the Doctor's son, and lives in the house where Billy was born. Jonnie and Billy are friends at school, loving the natural world and dreaming up all kinds of adventures together. Soon Billy and Jonnie catch up with Charlie and they run as fast as they can to be at the airstrip in time to see the plane fly low over the airstrip checking for obstructions. They can see the pilot looking down from his window before turning sharply to line up for a final approach. The boys join an excited crowd of onlookers as the plane throttles back, almost gliding onto the airstrip before a final surge of power gives it the smooth landing that everyone admires. It taxis the final hundred yards, bouncing and jolting on the rough grass, and then turns sharply to park at the edge of the strip, right by the track where everyone is waiting eagerly. Dr Mote arrives in his Landrover to welcome Mr. Brown and whisks him off. Billy knows that this will probably mean setting off for home tomorrow.

He and Jonnie crouch on the grass in the morning sunshine and watch an African friend of Jonnie's called Benjamin who is bashing small pegs made out of sticks into the ground underneath the plane to make a rough, full-sized outline. An hour later after the plane has taken off, Benjamin is carefully measuring the length and width of the wings and fuselage. He scales it down to come up with an accurate drawing he is making with a stubby pencil in his school exercise book. Over the next few days Benjamin constructs a scale model of the plane made entirely out of wire and some clear plastic he has found, based on his drawing. This becomes the most sought after toy on the mission station. Benjamin has even found a small frog who has been pressed into service as the pilot. He sits indignantly in the cockpit of the wire Cessna.

Billy's cloud is a little bigger and a little darker as he climbs into the car next morning. Charlie has had his x-ray showing that he is fit enough to start school. The journey home is long and hot, and Billy hardly notices the butterflies by the river at rest hour. He is glad when the car moves off the section of road that runs alongside huge electric pylons and heads directly south. Now there is only the village of Kabweba to go before reaching home.

Chapter 9

Billy's dad notices it first. "There's no one out today, I wonder what's going on. Even the fields are empty. No one's working."

The little village is like a ghost town. The breeze picks up little eddies of dust, spinning them and then letting them go. Unusually there are no people to be seen anywhere.

"Something's wrong". Faith's face is full of concern.

Then out from the last hut comes King George, obviously distressed. His face is tear-stained. He waves his arms frantically to stop the car, and practically drags the family out, guiding them to the shade and safety of the first hut where he lives with his family. The village chief is sitting on a chair. Everyone else is seated on the floor, or on small, animal skin stools. Bella, King George's sister begins:

"We give thanks to God that you were not here two hours ago! White soldiers came. They landed at Mutshatsha. There has been shooting and burning at Kalemba village. They came to your house and have taken some things. They were looking for you."

"Granny! Is Granny safe?" Faith holds Bella's arm a little too tight.

"Rhonda was with her. The soldiers did not go into her house. They are safe. Rhonda has stayed with her, King George ran here so that he could warn you before you arrived at your home."

Billy moves closer to his dad. Charlie looks frightened.

"Thank God the x-ray machine wasn't working when we arrived at Kasaji! We would have come home yesterday!" says Faith.

"Are the soldiers still around?" asks John.

"No, they have gone now. We heard the plane fly out about an hour ago. There are injured people at the hospital."

Faith is on her feet. "We must go." She says urgently.

"First we must pray". Every head is bowed. "Father, thank you for your timing and protection today. Thank you that you have spared our lives. We pray that you will be very close to those who are bereaved or injured.

Help us to bring healing and comfort. Please protect us all from evil and harm."

King George wants to travel into Mutshatsha Mission with the Walkers. John and Faith are deep in thought, asking themselves questions they will only discuss once the boys are asleep. It is only just over twenty four hours before missionaries from all over Katanga will arrive at Mutshatsha with their children, ready to set off in convoy across the border into Zambia and the school. This journey can be dangerous at the best of times, but now the danger has increased. They will be able to discuss this with Kasaji and other missions on the mission radio network.

From a distance the house looks normal. The car swings up onto the drive and the boys jump out.

"Wait, let me go in first!" Billy stops and takes firm hold of Charlie's hand. They watch as their dad disappears into the house. Mum stands with the boys until Dad comes back out. He kneels in front of them.

"The door is broken, but most of our things are still here. They have taken the radio and cleared out the pantry, so there is not much food, but it could be a lot worse. We are all safe, and that's what really matters".

"There are forty five people arriving to eat and sleep tomorrow. We have nothing to feed them, and no means of contacting them. We can't put them off." Faith looks anxious.

"God has brought us this far safely. We must ask him to provide what we need, and to keep us safe." Still kneeling, John gathers his family into a circle. They hold hands.

"Father, thank you that most of our things are safe. You know what our needs are right now. We pray that you will provide a way for us to replace the radio, and Jesus, you fed five thousand with almost nothing, please help us to feed forty five people tomorrow. Please keep us all safe."

Charlie has already slipped away. He is running around to Granny's house. By the time Billy arrives, he is knocking on the door. Granny's face appears at the window. She is holding a stout broomstick.

"Oh it's you Charlie dear! You have no idea how pleased I am to see you! Come in, come in."

Dad arrives. Mum is already on her bike, pedaling down to see what she can do at the hospital.

"Are you alright Granny?" Dad follows the boys into her little sitting room, which is bedecked with pictures painted all over central Africa and some of Natal in South Africa; paintings from visits to her brother.

"Of course I'm alright, why wouldn't I be?" she says indignantly! " Rhonda and I could hear shooting. At first we thought someone had brought some fireworks from the Copper Belt, but Rhonda could remember the shootings during the fight for independence. She was only a little girl. She was sure it was guns, so we locked ourselves in the toilet with a broomstick. The shooting got closer, and then we heard someone banging on the door of the main house, and shouting "Walker, Walker, open up!" After a while they began to kick the door, until they were inside. We could hear doors slamming and heavy boots. They didn't stay long, and then it was quiet. After about half an hour we heard the plane starting up, and we knew they were leaving. Thank God you weren't here!"

"We have", says John, sitting back in Granny's basket work sofa. Rhonda brings some tea in, but she is crying.

"Are you alright Rhonda?" John takes the tray.

"It's my family, Mr. Walker. I don't know what's happened to them. We live in Kalemba."

"Do you want to go to them?"

"No, I'm afraid of what I will find. Can I stay here?"

"Of course. Mrs. Walker will bring us news when she gets back from the hospital." John turns to the boys. "Don't go too far from the house".

Billy and Charlie are feeling shocked. They hate seeing Rhonda so upset. They are worried about Divine, her younger sister who comes up to play sometimes. She is twelve. The boys sit on the old log by the bath fire, only a few yards from Granny's door while the grownups carry on talking. Billy puts his chin in his hands and stares down at the dusty ground. Here and there he can see the funnels of ant-lion traps dug into the sand. They are designed so that ants that wander into them, find the sand giving way under their feet making it impossible for them to escape. Billy watches closely as one hapless ant struggles to get away. He knows what will happen. Within seconds the ant-lion who is hidden under the bottom of the trap in the sand, suddenly sends up two powerful pincers that drag the unfortunate ant underground where it will be eaten. Usually the whole drama fascinates Billy, but the school cloud has grown bigger, and now his last day at home has been spoilt too. He will not be able to complete his usual rounds, or go on a last butterfly hunt to all the shrubs and other plants he knows are just coming into flower.

Soon his world will be invaded by lots of other families, and children that he will be at school with. He is looking forward to seeing Jonnie again, but he is the kind of boy who stays on the edge of the crowd, and never wants to be at its centre. He has one or two good friends, and loves to be by himself, in his own little world. The thought of all those people and so many excited children fills him with gloom, especially as it heralds the inevitable start of another interminable term far away from his precious world. Far away from his precious mum and dad.

King George busies himself getting food ready for the evening meal. Even he is quiet today. Mum does not come back from the hospital at the usual time. Dad says grace and the boys tuck into sardines mixed up in tinned tomatoes with toast made from home-made bread. Nobody has much to say. Mum comes in as they are finishing their food. She looks pale and serious. She sits down at the far end of the table and bursts into tears. King George brings her some water and indicates that he is ready to bring in her food. She signs to King George not to bring her food yet.

"There is nothing left of Kalemba," she says, "they have burned it to the ground. Every hut has gone. Only three young women avoided getting shot. They were in the river when the attack came and swam under water to safety."

"Is Divine safe?" Billy's blue eyes are big and round. His face is pale. His mum slips out of her seat and comes close enough to take Billy and Charlie by the hand. Her eyes still full of tears.

"Her body is at the hospital. She is in heaven now." As she says this, Rhonda walks in. Mum turns to her. Rhonda collapses into her arms and sobs. King George brings more water.

Mum tries to find a way to tell Rhonda that her whole family has been shot, but she can't. She just says, "I'm so sorry, I'm so sorry." Dad carries her to the settee where she curls up and cries until she is exhausted.

Mum and Dad stare across the table at each other and then try to get the boys to eat. King George has worked out what is happening. He does not need words to understand the pain the family is feeling.

Then a cough at the door; the traditional way of being asked for permission to come in, like using a door bell. The door is already open to let cool air into the dining room. There on the doorstep is an old man, his face wizened by age, with a stubbly white beard. In one hand he has a piece of string which is attached at its other end to a well proportioned goat.

"Moyu eyi mwani." The old man stoops to bow as he goes through the ritual of greeting Dad, who continues the conversation on the doorstep, and by so doing, avoids adding a goat into an already complicated situation. Soon the conversation is over and Dad disappears around the back of the house to tie the goat to a low branch of the mulberry tree in the chicken run.

"What was all that about?" Mum is still comforting Rhonda.

"The old man has walked all the way from Nyangula. It must be twenty five miles by foot. The goat was a present."

"But why?"

"Do you remember that little girl, Precious, who had polio?"

Mum remembers her all too well. She first met Precious when she was two years old. She was lying in a ditch by the side of the road starving and dehydrated. She was barely alive. She had been left there by her heartbroken mother after the village spiritman had decided that she was possessed by an evil spirit because her legs weren't working properly, and had ordered that she should be thrown out of the village. Her mother prayed that someone would find her and rescue her, though this was very unlikely to happen. Anyone acting against the instructions of the spiritman was likely to come to an untimely end. Mum had brought her back to the hospital. On the way she decided her name should be Precious. At the hospital she had recovered to the point where she could be fostered by a family from the mission church. Eventually she had been to Lubumbashi to be fitted with some prosthetic legs and had started going to school, where she proved to be the brightest girl in her class. First she learned to get around with crutches, and then became so confident that she was able to walk unaided. When she was fifteen she returned to her village. The spiritman was dead, but her mother was too ashamed to have her back, so Precious had moved in with her grandparents.

"Now the old man has arrived with a thank you present. It has taken him a year to save up enough money to buy this handsome goat. Having delivered it, he has gone to sleep as the guest of a relative on the mission station."

Still crying, Mum laughs at this amazing answer to prayer. "I hope they all like goat stew", she says wiping her eyes.

Billy lies in bed, his eyes are still wide open in the dark. He is tired, but not sleepy. Somehow he feels safe, but there are so many things running through his mind. He can see Divine's face so clearly in his imagination. He remembers the water fight they had in the river the last time he saw her. He can't believe that she is gone. It seems so unfair.

"God, why did you answer our prayers by making us late and sending the goat, but let Divine die?" he whispers.

Chapter 10

Billy is aware of the big black cloud before he can remember why it is there! Then it all comes rushing back. The trauma of yesterday, and the prospect of a different invasion that is going to happen later today.

He eats his breakfast slowly, but his mind isn't following the Bible passage or the prayers, urgent as they are. Today his regular round will be turned into a series of goodbyes.

First he carries the fish tank out onto the lawn and places it carefully onto the grass. One by one he lifts the chameleons out onto the branch where he had found them. They have more than doubled their size. As if by magic they change colour from dark green to mottled grey, merging in with the bark of the poinsettia tree.

"Bye-bye little cammies" he says, "You will be grown up before I get home".

The flower border greets him with a blaze of colour. Some of the zinnias are still flowering and a multi-coloured host of snapdragon spires has risen up to join them. The praying mantis has moved on. Billy stops to just gaze at it all. "I'm going to miss you", he says wistfully.

Then on to find Lucy. She still has the look of an outraged school mistress, but now she is sitting on six large brown eggs. "Bye-bye Lucy. I hope I can be as brave as you", he says mournfully.

The dark shade of the mango tree seems to match Billy's mood. Whiskers curls up on Billy's lap instead of sitting on his shoulder, as if to seek comfort. Granny has not come out to paint. In the distance Billy can hear wailing. He knows that it is the sound of another funeral. Some one else must have died this morning.

Billy puts in an extra visit to see the goat, which is tied by a longer piece of string and is staked at the far end of the lawn, happily eating green grass. Billy is surprised at how strong she is.

During rest hour, Billy can hear the drone of the first plane coming in. He does not feel the urge to run up to see it land. Snowy is stretched out full length on the bed beside him. Billy strokes her tummy gently, watching her paws curl and uncurl. She purrs softly.

"It's alright for you," he says quietly. "You can stay here. What do you know about school?" She twitches an ear and goes back to sleep.

Preparations for supper are under way. The main course is still alive. Living on a small mission station means buying bush meat from local hunters or killing your own domestic animals. Charlie has grown used to being present at the slaughter of animals that will end up on the table, but Billy always makes sure he is far away when it happens. Once Charlie had persuaded him to attend when King George had beheaded a chicken, but Billy was horrified by the way it flapped around for nearly a minute without its head.

"That's the last time I'm going to watch that happen", he said as he stomped off into the house.

Sometime during the afternoon, the goat meets its end. King George is a very good cook, and Billy loves watching him turn raw ingredients into a tasty meal. The best bits of the goat have been diced and browned in two huge black saucepans. King George has lit another fire outside over which he has hung a large cauldron into which has gone water and the diced goat. Now he is throwing in lots of vegetables, seasoning and a whole chopped pineapple. Potatoes are being baked in the fire. By supper time Billy is starving. The children get to eat sitting on blankets on the lawn. Some tents have appeared too. There is not enough room for everyone to sleep in the house or the guest house a hundred yards beyond Granny's house.

Slowly a hush settles on the mission station, but there is not the usual excitement. Everyone is shocked at the mercenaries' attack, and quietly, when the children are not around, they discuss the dangers of tomorrow's journey.

Chapter 11

The generator grinds into action at 4.30am. Tents are packed away in the dark. Families sit around on the veranda sipping hot tea or Milo. Everyone is whispering so as not to wake anyone, but everyone is on the move.

By six o'clock everyone is ready to go. Pedro has come up from Mutshatsha Gare with his old truck to get in some of the passengers who have arrived by plane. Billy sticks his nose to the window and watches the mist rising on the Kalemba river as the Zephyr cautiously edges across the loose planks on the bridge. The scene is so tranquil. This river is his friend. How many hours has he spent splashing and jumping from the bridge, or standing stock still in the refreshing water, net ready to scoop up a fish. He feels sad as the river disappears behind him.

The road passes through what is left of Kalemba village. Now for the first time the true extent of the horror can be seen. All the bodies have been removed and buried. There is not a single hut still standing, though some of the lathes and supports form grotesque twisted sculptures, and are still smoking. A tall wooden manioc bowl lies on its side, abandoned, a child's shoe, and the charred remains of a dog. Billy wants to see, and yet he desperately wants not to see. There is nothing left except ashes, where Rhonda, Divine and her family used to live. Billy feels numb and sick at the same time. His mum turns and takes him by the hand. There is nothing she can say.

Two miles down the road, there is another small village, which from the car looks as if it is carrying on as usual. People are busy sweeping and pounding. The contrast is too much for Billy. He bursts into tears. His mother turns to wipe his eyes and Billy can see that she is crying too. Five more miles brings them to Mutshatsha Gare. The morning market is getting under way and the convoy stops to buy drinks and fruit to eat on the journey.

The Walkers buy a pineapple from a young man called Amoni. He and his young wife, Luba are about to move to Lubumbashi where Amoni has secured a job working in the copper mine. "This is our last day running the market stall" he announces proudly.

"We will miss you both", says Billy's dad. He takes Amoni by the hand and prays for their future, and then with a big smile everyone says good bye and jumps back into the car.

A man is standing with a red flag at the railway crossing to show that a train is coming. Billy can hear it before he can see it, and then suddenly the huge steam engine, black and smoky rumbles across the track right in front of the car. The wheels are struggling to grip as the train builds up momentum. Steam and smoke surge out from every gap and pipe. There is a deep rumbling chuff, chuff, chuff, and the roar of an internal furnace. Billy thinks this is even more wonderful than watching a plane land. After the engine, comes the coal tender, and as it passes the engine lets out a loud hiss and then a whistle. Charlie puts his finger over his ears: "It's alive" he whispers, screwing up his face to keep it away.

Billy watches as the passenger carriages pass. First class passengers sit proudly in their seats fanning themselves. Second class is much more crowded. On the roof and hanging off the outside of the train are people who have not paid. They are banking on the ticket collector not checking up on them. As long as there are enough paying passengers, no one seems to mind, and there is no tunnel this side of Dilolo on the Angolan border, so everyone is relatively safe, as long as they hold on tight.

The road runs away from Mutshatsha Gare running almost due south towards The North West province of Zambia. The track is not used much apart from carrying children to school so the convoy moves slowly. By lunch time it has reached the Mukulweji River. This has been a strategic point every time war has broken out, since here is the only bridge over a significant river on the only road connecting the east west highway in southern Katanga with Zambia. Removing the bridge adds on a three hundred mile detour, and so effectively stops the movement of vehicular traffic between Katanga and Zambia across a huge area.

The river is littered with the remains of earlier bridges that have been destroyed. The current bridge, rebuilt recently with crude pillars made from drums filled with cement, some iron pieces of train rail, and then on top some sleepers. Disconcertingly, some of the sleepers have been removed for fire wood, and those that remain are not all tied down. The convoy stops here for lunch and to inspect the bridge before the first vehicle, Mr. Rew's Landrover cautiously makes its rattling way to the other side.

Billy crouches on a rock looking over the river, munching on a corned beef sandwich. He is scanning the river bank opposite. Sure enough, basking in the midday sun he can see an old crocodile. He does not flinch even with all the hubbub, on and around the bridge. And there in a still patch of water Billy can see the eyes and back of another one, a little smaller.

"They are waiting for someone to fall in." he says to Charlie who is crouching beside him.

The Zephyr is wider than most of the other cars, so Dad gets mum to walk across with the boys, "Just in case!"

Billy has never been good with heights, so he finds the walk across the bridge with no side rails quite scary, especially when they have to step over gaps or walk on loose planks. He is pleased to get to the other side, but his school cloud gets a little bigger. He always feels he is closer to school than to home once he gets across the Mukulweji River.

Amazingly all eight vehicles are still running. Oil and water has been topped up, and the convoy heads up the hill away from the river and through another large village. This is the hottest part of the day. There is almost no one out in the village, but this is not unusual.

Charlie is fast asleep, his head back and his mouth wide open. Billy is also dozing despite the bumping and swerving of the car. Thick dark shadows crisscross the road from tree braches above. Pedro's truck is just in front. It bumps up and over a ridge in the road, which turns out to have a large head and tail! Now its head is up a full two feet above the road. The car swerves, Billy wakes up with a start just in time to see the rock python slithering and writhing away into the bush on his side of the car.

"Did you see that Dad! It's still alive!"

The border is marked by a small shack with the word Arrêter painted in large black letters on its whitewashed wall, and a flimsy metal bar counterbalanced with a rock to make it easy to open or close. There is no sign of anyone manning the border as the first Landrover pulls up. The driver jumps out and begins to call for attention, whereupon two men in uniform, carrying rifles slung across their shoulders amble out from behind some shady trees. Their faces light up as they see the convoy, as this is the first traffic they have encountered for a very long time. They refuse to speak to anyone until they are properly seated inside their office, have put their hats on and have opened the shutters to the outside world. The drivers gather around with passports and licenses in hand, ready to have them stamped. The customs official gathers them into two neat piles, well inside their little booth.

"Pour chaque personne je nécessitera cent francs", he says firmly, whilst brushing imaginary crumbs from his uniform.

Everyone knows that the correct fee is ten francs per person, not one hundred, but pointing this out directly to the customs officials is unlikely to generate a positive outcome. The documents are very firmly in their possession, giving them a strong bargaining position. The missionaries have come to realise over the years that John Walker is the best diplomat amongst then, so they quietly make way for him to step forward. He conducts his conversation in French.

"Good day sir, my name is John Walker". He reaches out his hand to shake with both officials, a warm smile on his face. Faith walks quietly up behind him with a packet of Fox's Glacier Mints, and slips them onto the counter. It is fifty miles to the closest sweet shop. "We are here today with our children. They are travelling to school." John turns to find Billy and Charlie amongst the hopeful crowd of on-looking missionaries. He beckons them to his side. "This is my son Billy", he announces, looking proudly at him. "And this is Charlie". He lifts him up so that Charlie is high enough to reach across the counter and shake hands with both melting officials. Charlie's smile has been known to win the day on previous occasions.

"And how are your families", asks John with the air of a man who has all day to listen. The missionaries drift off to sit in their cars or on a nearby log. They know that this will take time. Billy seizes the opportunity to run off with his butterfly net, hoping to conduct a brief audit on the local flora and fauna, and to check all the radiator grills for good specimens.

Twenty minutes later, and one of the officials finishes his summary of the health and wellbeing of his family by confiding in John that his oldest son is working as a third member of the customs team (Clearly two are not enough for the heavy work load generated by one or two border crossings each week). He is working as a volunteer. Not asking for any wages. He is doing this as an act of service to his country, but right now he has a terrible headache.

John turns to Faith, who after a very brief conversation retrieves a half empty tin of stripy gold and black humbugs from the car. Billy loves these. They are saved for long journeys. He looks on in horror as his mum strides off towards the customs booth with them. By now the customs men have taken off their hats and are wandering off down a dusty path either side of John, who has his arms around their shoulders. Faith catches up and they disappear into the cool darkness of a thatched hut. A young man is lying with a cloth covering his eyes. The hut smells strongly of beer, and the table on one side of the room shows evidence of a hard night's drinking. Faith kneels gently at his side, removing the cover from his eyes. The young man groans and turns his face away from the light.

"I have seen this kind of headache before. Give him plenty of water to drink, and give him one of these every four hours until he is well". She plants the tin of humbugs beside his pillow, prises off the lid and extracts one humbug. She indicates to the young man to sit up, plumping up his pillow as if he is the star patient in the hospital back at Mutshatsha. She asks him to open his mouth and places the humbug on his tongue. The young man sinks back onto his bed, already looking better, and the whole party returns to the customs office. One of the officials emerges from the office and starts to hand out the documents in exchange for exactly ten francs per person. In no time at all the barrier has swung up, and the convoy pass through with many smiles and much waving.

Billy's butterfly hunt proved to be fruitless. "Now I'm in Zambia," he thinks to himself, leaning his arms on the seat in front of him. He closes his eyes and breathes in deeply, savouring the scent of his mother. He leans forward a little more and wraps his arms around his mum, leaning his head on her shoulder, he sighs. Neither of them say anything, but the cloud is not only growing bigger and darker, it feels as if it is getting lower. Faith tries not to show that a tear has crept into one eye. She knows Billy's scent too. She wonders how she will cope without her precious boys running around her feet, and driving King George mad! She has her own cloud, and it is getting bigger too. For a long time Billy will not let her go. Charlie is quiet too, feeling the change in atmosphere.

Soon they pass quickly though another small village. They hardly notice it. A little girl called Ruby plays happily in the sun whilst her mother rests after a hard morning working in the fields.

Quite suddenly a rickety bridge presents itself to the convoy, carrying the vehicles over a small, playful, fast-running river about five metres across. John turns to the boys. "That's the Zambezi River. When it has grown very big it will go over the Victoria Falls, remember?"

Billy can remember. He was only five when the family took the train from Lubumbashi all the way down to Cape Town. It was the biggest adventure ever! The engine was like a big monster or a dragon. It seemed to be alive, and Billy had first met it in the dark. It seemed angry. Black and yet glowing with fire, and hissing with steam and smoke. Its huge wheels slipping and spinning as it tried to find traction. The carriage on the other hand, offered some comfort. Bouncy seats that you could jump up and down on (when your mum and dad had gone off down the corridor), and a sink to wash in or just to splash water on your face; real luxury!

The journey had taken a whole week. One night Dad had looked at his watch, and thinking it was ten past eight, hurried to get Billy and Charlie ready for breakfast in the restaurant car. It was only when he was pushing them down the corridor, that he looked at the time again to see that he had read his watch upside down! Instead of being ten past eight, it was twenty to two in the morning! By this time Charlie, aged only three, was determined to get the breakfast he felt he was owed, and when his dad picked him up and began taking him back along the corridor, he screamed and kicked so loudly, that everyone in both first-class carriages was awake, and most of them had their heads out in the corridor to see what was happening. Billy was looking out of the window at the miracle of the Milky way splashed across the sky, and diamond stars flashing so brightly, that he felt he could reach out and catch them in his hand.

Dad looked very sheepish when breakfast really did arrive, and Billy could not understand why everyone was frowning at them.

Then there was the Victoria Falls. The train had pulled slowly onto the bridge. One second the family was staring out into the familiar bush of the newly independent Zambia, the next second the ground had dropped away, more than four hundred feet below them to churning grey-blue water running down a narrow gorge. There in front of them was the awesome sight of the world's largest sheet of falling water. It was majestically breathtaking. The spray from the falls quickly misted up the windows, so that John had to pull them open to reveal the true splendour of the view. The deep thunder of three thousand tonnes of water per second could not only be heard, but it could also be felt, adding an extra shudder to the movement of the old engine as it hissed and belched it's way across the bridge. The train had stopped on the Rhodesian side of the bridge long enough for a walk. Billy remembers that the Victoria Falls has its own delicate gladioli, unfurling lemon yellow flowers which grow right on the edge of the cliffs. He remembers that where the spray is heavy and constant and there is plenty of shade, wild African violets grow in rich velvety cushions which hold water droplets away from the delicate centres of the plants with their deep purple flowers dotted with bright yellow stamens.

It is hard to believe that this sparkling, crystal stream the Zephyr is now crawling over, will turn into something so terrifyingly powerful.

The sight of the Zambezi means that somewhere behind them they have crossed imperceptibly over the watershed that runs from west to east across this part of central Africa. It divides the streams that rise and flow north into the great Congo basin, covering an area the size of Western Europe. The Congo River will disgorge all its collected water into the Atlantic Ocean. The stream they have just crossed which will flow south into another catchment area the same size, dominated by the Zambezi which will eventually flow in the opposite direction from the Congo, to empty itself into the Indian Ocean through a great delta system.

Except for one stop to refill a boiling radiator with cool water, for the first time John can remember, there have been no breakdowns and the convoy turns out of the long grass and across the end of the school airstrip as the late afternoon sun begins to dip below the low iron roofs of the school.

Chapter 12

Billy hates the way he feels. The cloud has enveloped him. Without knowing it a protective shell begins to form around him, one that he will use to try and hide his emotions. His face loses its softness. Under no circumstance must he let anyone know how his heart is breaking, or how desperately he wants to go home with his mum and dad. He had cried when he was younger, but that had backfired. The older children had looked disdainfully at him. It was soon made clear to him by staff members, that tears were not acceptable. He was told to pull up his socks. He couldn't understand how that would make him feel any better.

The school is centred round a big patch of bare ground called the play ground. It runs across a gentle slope. On the high side is a long single-story building with two wings. Looking from the play ground, the left wing is the girl's dormitory and the right wing is the boy's. In between is a staff house, creating a proper gap between the two. The play ground is surrounded by staff houses set back among the trees, and a school hall. Another larger building built around a concrete play area has four classrooms, a library and a small tuck-shop. Another building has a kitchen and dining room, and to complete the circle, there is a sickbay and living quarters for the school nurse. There are a few other buildings set a little further away from the play-ground, and half a mile away, in the loop of a small river there is a wild play area with a swimming pool and changing rooms. This is the only place where Billy does not feel the cloud.

Not everyone seems to have a cloud. Some of the children arrive and run off with friends to play, easily transferring to school life, but some, especially the very young ones look pale and stick close to their parents. To Billy, this is the worst time ever. He knows that his mum and dad are there at the school somewhere. They will not start the journey home until the following day, but they are whisked off to drink tea and eat cake in the staffroom where the children are not allowed.

Charlie is allocated a big boy to show him where his bed is, and to show him around.

Billy drags his case to the boy's dormitory block. The wing contains four open dorms off a wide corridor. There is a peg with his name on it and a number 11. He knows the number will relate to the number of his bed, and his own tiny bit of personal space. There is no ceiling. The corrugated iron roof is very hot at rest-hour, and very loud whenever there is a tropical downpour in the wet season. Billy has a bed with a mosquito net rolled away above it. He has an aisle between his bed and the one next to him. There is a wooden chair by his bedhead where he must put his case. He will be in trouble if the contents become untidy. There is nowhere else to put his clothes except his hook in the corridor where he will hang his mac, so his case is the only place to keep all his clothes and personal possessions. He carefully stands his precious butterfly net behind his case.

The dorm is completely open with five beds either side and an alcove at the end with four more beds. There are no partitions between the beds, so that although each boy gets his own bed and aisle space, there is no privacy at all. It smells slightly of disinfectant.

Jonnie Mote's bed is opposite Billy. Jonnie quickly arranges his case, and then trots off to the girl's wing where he sticks his head around the door to make sure his sister is being looked after.

Billy sits on his bed, his arms around his knees, and rocks gently as tears begin to fill his eyes. He wipes them away quickly, just as Mike Boden appears in the corridor and heads towards the hooks to find out his number. Mike is Billy's best friend at school. His family lives in Kitwe on the Zambian Copper Belt, so they never see each other in holiday times. Billy's face lights up when he finds out that Mike has the bed next to his, and for a while the cloud lifts as they chat about the past two months at home. Extra to his case, Mike has a cardboard box which he carries in carefully and places on Billy's bed. Very slowly he lifts up the flaps on the top of the box. Inside there is a deep layer of dry grass, and in the corner, rolled up tight, is a ball of fur which gently expands and contracts as it breathes. Disturbed by the light it lifts its head to show two enormous liquid brown eyes, and delicate ears which twitch tentatively.

"A bush-baby! You've brought a bush-baby!" Billy's eyes are nearly as large as the little creature staring up at him. "What's his name?"

"Walter."

"Where did you get him?"

"His mum was eaten by Lucy, the lady who cleans our house. Walter was tiny when his mum was caught. There was not enough meat on him to eat, so she brought him to me. He was so tiny that we had to feed him milk with a pipette, and then we started to mash up some squidgy caterpillars with some milk and feed him from the end of a spoon. Now he can eat whole grasshoppers, but his favourite is moths. He only likes eating when it's dark."

"Where's he going to live? You can't keep him in that box. Matron will never let you keep him in the dorm."

"Dad's already sorted it. Walter's allowed to live in the aviary,"

The aviary was only built last term, and of course was intended for birds. It consists of a stout wire cage set under some trees at one end of the playground. It is about eight feet wide, twelve feet long, and eight feet high. There is a little door at one end. A dead branch brought down by lightning is propped up diagonally from end to end making a robust perch. So far it has been used by a menagerie of small animals, but no birds. There are three wooden bird-boxes fixed hopefully in the uppermost regions of the aviary. These make ideal bush-baby homes.

Without another word Billy and Mike hurry out of the main entrance to the dormitories and across the playground where they are joined by Jonnie, to introduce Walter to his new home. They are surprised to find that a very European-looking rabbit has already taken up residence. He will not be a threat to Walter as he will spend his time on the ground, and bush-babies spend their entire lives off the ground. Mike carefully transfers the dry grass into a bird-box whilst Billy holds Walter, still asleep, against his shirt. Moments later Walter, unbeknown to him, has a new home.

"He's going to wonder where he is when he wakes up," says Jonnie. "We'll have to make sure we catch lots of insects for him."

A bell rings to announce supper time. Without saying anything, the boys run to the wash-room to clean their hands. They meet up with Charlie who is still being looked after by Patrick, an American boy who is taking his job as "buddy" very seriously. Charlie can only just reach his arms into the sink. They all run across the playground to line up outside the boy's door for the dining-room. The boys crowd around a list taped to the doorframe which tells them where they will be sitting. Billy is dismayed to find that he is not sitting with Mike or Charlie, and Miss Brotherton's name is written boldly at the top of the list of people sitting at his table. He is frightened of Miss Brotherton. She is a small lady, with piercing eyes, and a permanent intense look. To Billy she always seems to be on the edge of an angry outburst. Woe betide anyone who is late, or forgets something. The smallest thing can send her into a fit of rage, and then she will call her victim out in front of everyone, slip off one of her hard-soled shoes and beat them so hard that she nearly falls over. Billy is more afraid of the anger than the shoe. A cold sweat breaks out when Billy remembers how Miss Brotherton had written the date on the board in a literature lesson last year for the class to copy. Billy has never been good at spelling, and he copied down "February" wrongly. Miss Brotherton marched up and down the aisles between the desks stopping to make sure each child had written their name and the date correctly at the top of their paper. The class held its breath, frightened that someone might have got it wrong.

"Billy Walker," she shrieked suddenly. "Why do I waste my time writing things on the board for you to copy? Come out here!" Her shoe was already off. "Bend over." The only funny thing was that she hit Billy so hard standing on the one foot still wearing a shoe, that her other foot flew out behind her kicking a desk, and leaving her hopping around frantically whilst Billy tried his hardest to regain his composure, and not to cry in front of the class.

A hush falls on the dining room as Mr. Birch, the head teacher, walks into the room. He is a slightly portly man with a shock of white hair and a complexion that betrays his mood. Whenever he is angry, which seems to Billy like most of the time, his face quickly turns bright red like a cockerel. When Mr. Birch has his red face, it is definitely best not to be seen or heard! His glasses sit a little too far down on his nose, adding to a sense that he too might explode into a fit of rage at any moment. Billy stands quietly behind his chair waiting for grace to be said. Mr. Birch bangs on the table with the handle of his knife three times. Silence quickly follows, grace is said and the meal begins. Billy loves his food and when it is time for his table to get seconds, he lines up eagerly. He is relieved to find that there is still some rice and corned beef hash. Billy pours a liberal helping of what he thinks is gravy over his rice, only to find out that he has actually poured chocolate sauce on it. He does not dare to tell Miss Brotherton about his mistake, so without giving anything away, he eats the unlikely mixture and leaves an empty plate.

The African night falls very quickly. From the staff-house steps, comes the familiar "All in" call. Everyone stops what they are doing and runs in to the dormitories to get ready for bed. First the young ones and then the older children gather in a common room to listen to a bedtime story.

Billy is not listening. This is a time for him to go into his own little world, the one mentioned by his form teacher, Miss Stafford, when summing up in his school report last term: "Billy lives in a world of his own, and rarely pays proper attention in class."

His mind begins to drift home. He wonders what King George is doing, and imagines fishing for mudfish in a deep pool with Rubeni.

The cloud has settled over Billy again. It is bed time and he has not seen his mum and dad. Have they already left for home without telling him? Will they be allowed to say goodbye to him? He stands on his bed to undo his mosquito net which he then tucks in all round his bed except for one side so that he can crawl in. Although you can see through the net, it helps to provide an almost private space.

The lights are out and nobody dares to talk, even after the clip-clop of the matron's shoes has disappeared down the corridor. Suddenly Billy feels desperately lonely. A wave of homesickness sweeps over him like a tide, and he turns his head into his pillow and cries quietly until sleep begins to come.

There is a gentle hand on Billy's shoulder. Billy wakes and turns his head to see the silhouette of his mother kneeling beside his bed in the dark. His father is standing beside her. He loosens the mosquito net enough to sit on the edge of the bed and takes Billy's hand.

"Good night darling, I love you." His mum whispers into his ear, and gives him a long hug. Billy says nothing, thinking that if he tries to speak, they will know he is crying. He tries to be brave.

"Keep an eye on Charlie." whispers his dad. Billy squeezes his hand, and then they are gone.

Billy knows that they are saying goodbye, not goodnight. His heart is broken again, and he wonders how long it will take to mend. By morning his pillow is wet with tears. He turns it over so no one will see.

Chapter 13

The wake-up bell goes at 6.15am and Billy takes a few seconds to remember where he is. He sits on the edge of his bed for a few moments remembering that final hug, but he does not have time to dwell on it. The breakfast bell will go in half an hour.

Breakfast is Billy's favourite meal of the day, providing two of his very favourite things to eat; rice cakes and Marmite. The rice cakes are made into egg-sized balls and pan fried from soggy rice that is boiled and then left overnight to mulch. On Wednesdays and Thursdays for a treat there are sardines and tomato sauce mixed to a paste instead of Marmite. Billy loves this too.

Miss Stafford eyes her class with a stern face over horn rimmed glasses as her little flock files into the room, one by one, and in silence. She is holding a stout wooden ruler in her hand. She does not use it for measuring. Everyone knows it is her way of reminding the class that she will not tolerate any misbehaviour. Billy chooses a seat at the back of the class, where he hopes he will not be noticed. The first lesson is history.

Miss Stafford does not need to ask the class to settle down. There is no greeting, and no small talk, just a formal prayer while everybody stands, and then straight to the subject in hand.

"This term we will be studying the kings and queens of England. I'm looking for someone who can name a monarch and give me a notable fact about the one they have chosen." She walks up and down the aisle, letting her question sink in, and giving her pupils time to think.

The only King, Billy can think of is King George, and he is fairly sure Miss Stafford will not understand if he tells her how he taught him to eat roasted caterpillars! As for the other kings and queens of England, apart from a few pictures of past royalty, making them look like aliens from another planet, Billy knows nothing. By now he is staring out of the window. It's Wednesday, and that means time at the river this afternoon. In his day-dream Billy is already there, rushing to a pool that he and Mike found last term which was full of tiny tadpoles.

Miss Stafford has to say his name twice before Billy realises she is speaking to him. That is once too many!

"Put out your hand Billy Walker." Billy holds out his hand. He closes his eyes. Three sharp whacks with the heavy ruler sting the palm of his left hand. Billy grits his teeth. He must not cry. Within seconds his hand is swollen and throbbing.

Having completed her introduction, Miss Stafford proudly unveils a chart showing all the monarchs of England from Alfred the Great in AD 871 to Queen Elizabeth the second.

"Open your exercise books and copy them out carefully. I want your best hand writing."

Desk lids clatter as each person reaches inside to find their exercise book and a pencil. He knows that the lines on the page are straight and evenly spaced, but to Billy, they always seem to dance and quiver, as if they are mocking him. It always takes him longer to write because he has to check he has put each letter in the right order, and then he often muddles them up. He checks as carefully as he can but finds it hard to spot the mistakes.

Today Billy has another problem. His left hand is now so swollen that he can't grip his pencil. He knows better than to expect any sympathy, but he thinks putting up his hand to tell the teacher will generate less grief than simply not doing what he has been told to do. He holds up his right hand.

"What's the matter Billy Walker, didn't I make the instructions clear?"

"Please Miss, I can't hold my pencil."

"You are a stupid boy for giving me your left hand, and if you think this is going to get you out of copying the list, you have another think coming. You can sit quietly until morning break, and then you can come back after supper tonight to complete your work."

At break time Billy runs a basin of cold water and plunges his hand into it. The throbbing begins to go down.

Chapter 14

The first good thing about Wednesday afternoon is the tuck-shop. Billy waits in line, excited at the prospect of spending his five *ngwee* on Refreshers and a huge gobstopper. The latter will last him right through rest-hour and the whole afternoon, running out conveniently, a little before supper. It will turn his tongue blue, then black and finally purple as it shrinks through all its layers. The Refreshers will be locked away in the sweet cupboard where Billy has his own jar. He is saving these for half-term.

Rest hour is a time for reading, and although he is not in his own room, and Snowy is not there to share it with him, Billy finds comfort in his gobstopper and his book which provides him with free passage back into the tropical rain forests of the Cameroon.

As soon as the bell goes, there is a mad rush to the tables, set up outside the dining room. Here there is sponge cake topped with garishly coloured icing, and tea, fuel for a long, happy afternoon by the river. Still munching his cake, Billy and his friends walk slowly back to the dorm to fetch a towel and trunks. Shoes and socks are removed and placed tidily under beds. They will not be needed for a few hours. Billy grabs his net, and all three sit on the dorm steps waiting for the whistle. The path winds its way gently down the hill for half a mile through the school grounds and some bush before widening out into an open area, dotted with trees, that has been a happy, wild playground for two generations of children.

The first hour is spent swimming. The pool has been filled by diverting water along a channel from the river, and it is nearly full. Mr. Roberts wanders around the pool checking that it is not already being used by any other wildlife. Sometimes a snake or a monitor lizard needs to be scooped out before the children are allowed in. Satisfied, Mr. Roberts gives the "all clear" and the calm water suddenly turns into a happy, tea-coloured, churning turmoil of noise and fun.

Charlie is a "non-swimmer", but he will not be for long. Patrick has already wrapped him round with a bicycle inner tube, which makes him look like he has fallen victim to a small boa-constrictor. He is standing nervously with his contemporaries, waiting to get into the shallow end for doggy-paddle lessons. Billy has his hard earned red and blue swimming seals already, which means he can swim anywhere in the pool.

Swimming is followed by free time. Billy is in such a hurry to dress before Jonnie and Mike that he forgets to change his costume for his pants, and just pulls his shorts on over the top of his trunks. Net in hand, he is the first to reach the river. Billy loves everything about it. The dark shady trees which bow and stoop over it in places, the pools where the water moves slowly and the fish are biggest, the rapids with their constant chatter and babble, the island, a safe sanctuary from the younger children who are too scared to cross over to it.

The dam the boys built last term has been eroded back to the bare rocks and stones that were used to give it structure. All the gravel and mud that made it secure as a fish pond has been washed away by wet season floods, so the first job is to renovate and reconstruct. Then some big rocks are brought in along with some weed to make it suitable for new residents. At last the boys can start fishing. Billy's net gets the first catch. Jonnie and Mike are using a handkerchief. Jonnie holds two corners, and Mike, the other two. They scoop it under an overhanging part of the bank and bring up tadpoles with strong hind legs, almost ready to turn into frogs.

For two hours, Billy's world is cloudless.

There is free time after supper, but this is also the time when any misdemeanours must be paid for. The most common punishments for minor offences are "marching" or writing lines. On most evenings, one or more children are seen walking briskly around the edge of the playground, the circumference being about a hundred and fifty metres. Marching is annoying, but otherwise not to be feared. Billy prefers this to writing lines, which always takes him much longer than anyone else. Any more serious crime will result in a beating of some kind. Some teachers use their own footwear, like Miss Brotherton, whilst some choose to use the "paddle". This is a wooden bat about twice the size of a table tennis bat, made from a heavy African hardwood.

Billy remembers that the kings and queens of England are waiting patiently to be copied into his exercise book. Before running back to his class to complete his work he catches Jonnie. During free time a member of staff will appear on the staff house steps to give out post. A big crowd gathers, eager to get their first letter from home.

"Can you get my post" Billy calls.

"Sure" Jonnie calls over his shoulder.

By the time Billy has finally added Queen Elizabeth the second, his hand, now recovered from the morning, is tired, and as he leaves the classroom, he can hear "All in" being called.

Billy looks enquiringly at Jonnie as they get ready for bed, but Jonnie shakes his head.

"There was no post at all from the Congo." he says.

As Billy is closing his case before tucking himself into bed, his Bible slides of the lid, and onto the floor. Whilst picking it up he notices it has fallen open to a page that his dad loves to read to him. It is Joshua chapter one. Whenever they have sat in bed together looking at stories from the Bible, his dad has used a pencil to underline the bits that he and Billy like most. On this page it is verse five: *"As I was with Moses, so I will be with you; I will never leave you nor forsake you."*

His heart still aching, Billy thinks about how Moses had run far away from his home and family, and how alone he must have felt. He feels as if God is reminding him that he is still there, even closer than his butterfly net! A gentle softness settles on him like a blanket, and wraps him up. A peace that dissolves the cloud, and lets him sleep.

Chapter 15

Every evening Billy stands with his friends, hoping for his name to be read out by the teacher with the post. Three weeks have gone by, and Mike has had three letters. Even Jonnie has had one from the Congo, but none has arrived for Billy. He is worried, because he is used to receiving a letter every week written and illustrated with little drawings by his mum. Each evening he wanders away after the last piece of post has been given out, to sit on a rock. All around him other children run off with their precious letters to read them with a close friend, or on their own.

And there is something else. Some of the other children from the Congo have heard rumours of more trouble across the border. Billy sits and stares at the floor, randomly drawing with a stick, his brow furrowed with anxiety, until he feels the tears building. At times like this he longs for someone to tell, someone who will give him a hug and assure him that everything will be fine, if only his mum was here, but there is no one.

Billy has a secret place that he goes to when he needs to shut out the world. At the opposite end of the classroom block from the tuck shop, there is a walk-in cupboard full of cleaning equipment, bottles of wax and detergent, brooms and polishers. This little room is never locked. There are some shelves that work well as steps and Billy has found that it is an easy way into the loft space above one of the class rooms. No one else comes here, and no one else knows that Billy comes here. Under one of the rafters he keeps a little note book where he writes down his secrets. The things he can't even tell Jonnie or Mike. Only Billy and God see what is written there. Here too Billy keeps a jar with any new butterflies he has caught. They are dried and ready to pin into boxes when he gets home at the end of term. This is the only place where he can be on his own, so while letters are being read, Billy runs across the playground, and disappears into the cleaning cupboard. He sits on a beam and cries, silently letting the tears roll down his cheeks. After a few minutes he pulls the little note book and a precious biro pen from its hiding place and carefully opens it to a new page. Slowly he begins to write:

Dear God,

I feel so lonely.
Please look after my mummy and daddy.
I wish they were here.

He stays for a long time in the quiet and the dark, until a little more gentleness seeps into his heart and makes him feel better.

The matron calls "All in". Billy scrambles down and runs up towards the dorm as the sun sinks quickly below the horizon casting long shadows across the playground.

Chapter 16

This is no ordinary Saturday, it is Billy's birthday. He wakes up with a sense of excitement, even though he has mixed feelings about birthdays. Before the rising bell the matron places birthday presents from home on the windowsill overlooking the dorm of the birthday boy. This comfortably avoids the awkwardness of matron actually handing it to him.

Billy's mum and dad usually bring a present with them at the beginning of term which matron then stores away until the big day. Any cards that arrive early are kept by her and brought out with the presents. Billy's one hope is that there will be a card, or something that will have arrived in the post, to assure him that his mum and dad are alright.

He can see that there is a brown paper package on the windowsill, and he knows that no one else in his dorm has a birthday today, so he jumps out of bed and runs to collect it. He picks it up carefully and looks around and under it, but there is no other post. Jonnie and Mike are already sitting on Billy's bed, excited to see what he has. He tears off the string and paper to find a green knitted long sleeved pullover, with a yellow "B" sewn onto the breast. Inside is a home-made card. It has a drawing of Lucy surrounded by little yellow chicks. Billy recognises his mother's artwork. It makes him smile. He holds the jumper up to his face and takes a long deep breath. It even smells like her.

Birthdays are the one day when Billy does not like breakfast. He knows that at some point Mr. Birch will bang his knife on the table, and in the silence that follows, he will be called upon to stand on his chair, while everyone will sing Happy Birthday to him. Billy hates the spotlight, and longs for this moment to be over, so that he can enjoy the day.

Saturday will mean an afternoon at the river, but there are classes in the morning. The first is "letters home". Billy sits twiddling his pencil as Miss Stafford strides up and down the aisles between desks. Billy knows the rules. His letter will be read by Miss Stafford before it is sent. No one is allowed to write anything negative in their letter "so as not to upset parents". He wishes he could say how worried and lonely he is, but he knows that if he does he will be back writing another letter in free time after supper, so he restricts himself to saying thank you for his pullover, which he is wearing proudly, and describing feeding time for Mike's bush-baby. This is his fourth letter home. He wonders if they are actually getting to his parents at all.

Something exciting is happening. The bell has gone for break and a crowd of children have gathered by a low wall running along one end of the playground. Billy runs to see what everyone is looking at. Mike has got there first. He turns to call to Billy as he runs. "Billy, come and look at this. It's a big snake!" Sure enough, there, laid out on the wall is a beautiful marked serpent, about six feet long, and as thick as a man's arm. Billy gasps when he sees it. He has never seen such an exquisite reptile in his whole life. It has a square-shaped head with large piercing eyes. Its skin is cream coloured with striking patterns in chocolate and beige.

"What is it?" whispers Billy, almost reverently.

Mr. Birch stands behind the wall. "This is a Gaboon Viper" he announces proudly. "It is claimed to be the largest venomous snake in the world, and its fangs can grow to two inches in length." He uses a stick to prize open the snake's mouth, showing two sets of double fangs. "It is a rare snake, and its venom is deadly."

"Wow! Can we pick it up Mr. Birch?"

"I think it will be too heavy, but if two of you come forward, and hold your arms out, I will lay it across you for a photograph."

Several boys scrabble to stand beside Billy, for the privilege of posing with the dead snake. Mike manages to fend off all the others, and soon he is standing with a broad smile on his face as Mr. Birch twists the camera lens into focus.

By the time the snake has been stroked, patted and admired, the bell is going for school again, and the beast is abandoned where it lies on the wall.

Billy is still only half way through copying out a new list of spelling words. Several people have finished already and sit gazing out of the window, when one of the boys stands up: "It's moving!" he says, pushing his nose against the glass to see better. There is the sudden sound of twenty five chairs being pushed back on the polished concrete floor, as the whole class rushes to the window. By this time the snake is slithering off the wall and making its way at great speed, its head slightly raised, tongue flicking in and out, across the playground and away between two buildings towards the bush. For a few moments, the whole class stands silently, taking in the implications of what they have just seen. Billy turns to look at Mike. They both look pale, but by lunch time they have become heroes for the day.

A lorry has arrived from the Copper Belt loaded with supplies, and carrying bundles of letters, held together with elastic bands. The usual crowds gather, hoping to get a letter from home. Billy does not join them. He sits on the rock within earshot, and tries not to build up his hopes. Without being seen, Charlie comes and sits on the rock beside him. He leans his head mournfully against his big brother's shoulder. They don't need to say anything. Soon all the letters have been given out.

The afternoon's adventures at the river and his worry about his parents fade as Billy lies in bed that night thinking about the snakes eyes, wide and unblinking, wondering whether they were watching him all the time.

Sunday is a day for dressing smartly and then trying to stay clean. In the dining room at lunch time there is a special treat. Above each place setting, two pieces of school fudge are placed. Billy tries to keep his for as long as possible, savouring the prospect of eating it as much as the blissful moment when he actually does eat it. His determination usually wears thin during rest hour, and it rarely lasts until river time.

Fudge is by far the most sought after currency in school. Almost anything can be swapped for it. Jonnie has given up both pieces for a Matchbox James Bond Aston Martin which fires red plastic missiles, and has a working ejector seat.

After supper on Sundays, there is a choice of two extra-curricular activities. Hymn singing or the lorry ride.

Billy loves the lorry ride. The cab of the S-type Bedford truck is pillar box red, and the radiator grill seems to be caught in a permanent smile. The back has low wooden sides and tailgate, with a loose metal frame fixed on top, over which a canvas cover can be attached. Mr. Roberts backs the lorry down to the turning circle, outside the sick-bay, and leaves the engine idling. It growls and rattles as the children clamber up into the back. The lorry makes its way up the road towards the airstrip, twisting and bobbing, rattling and bouncing whilst the children hold tight to the metal frame around them. Once across the airstrip the road comes to a "T" junction. A tall white sign gives the driver a choice of two directions. The sign pointing left reads "Mutshatsha". How Billy wishes Mr. Roberts would turn left and take him home across the border, but he always turns right along the road signposted to Hillwood Farm. At the right time of year, the lorry will stop and all the passengers will pile off to collect "shindwas"; small red, oval fruit, which stick out of the ground conspicuously. The fruit grow at the bottom of the plant which is part of the ginger family. Inside the leathery skin is white flesh, dotted with black pips. Billy loves the treasure hunt of finding them, but he regards them as too sharp for eating, so he keeps any that he finds until they go mouldy, and then throws them away. At home, his mother makes them into a delicious conserve, which to Europeans, tastes a lot like crab-apple jelly.

Billy, however, gets most excited in the months running up to Christmas, when flame lilies are out. The plants clamber and wind their stems around the surrounding vegetation until they are tall enough to produce stunning orange, red and yellow flowers which turn themselves inside out as they open, until the plant looks as if it as been decorated with individual little fires. Billy is proud of the fact that their local name of "Doctor's Joy" was coined by his great grandfather, a pioneer missionary and the founder of the school. Traditionally, Doctor's Joy is used for seasonal decoration in the absence of Christmas trees and tinsel. Billy teams up with Mike and Jonnie to gather as many as possible before the horn on the truck honks, calling them back to the lorry. The flowers are placed in a big jar on the dorm windowsill when they get back.

Billy's cloud has got bigger and lower every time he and Charlie fail to get a letter. When he is not occupied with the things he enjoys, he begins to day-dream. His mind wanders back across the border into the Congo, towards home. He catches glimpses of the ashes of Kalemba village. He thinks about Rhonda and Divine. He wonders why no news has come through. His day-dreams begin to steal into his sleep. Just before dawn one Sunday morning he dreams he is locked in the house with his Granny. He can hear the heavy thud of boots on the door, and the sound of shooting. He can smell the strange odour of burning that guns leave behind. There is a bang, and he wakes with a start. His head is sweaty, but the morning is cool.

Billy no longer enjoys his food. He pushes his lunch around his plate, in a world of his own, and forgets to take his fudge with him when Miss Brotherton finally announces to her table that they can be excused.

The lorry ride has lost its appeal.

"You go," he says dismissively to Jonnie and Mike as they run, full of excitement up to the truck as it backs, shuddering into its usual pick up spot. "I think I'll go to hymns today."

There is a semicircle of chairs set out around the piano in the school hall. Miss Stafford, without her ruler seems a little less frightening to Billy. He sits swinging his legs as small groups of girls come in and take their places. Some gather round the piano, helping to choose hymns. Billy is quiet. Although he knows the words to all the hymns, he has a frog in his throat, and does not want it to betray his emotions.

There is a feeling in the air; a kind of comfort. As if someone is wrapping an invisible blanket around Billy. It's a feeling he only has when he is with his mum, but it seems to have invaded the room with the hymns. It becomes almost unbearable, but Billy needs it so much. The tears well up and begin to trickle down his face. He wipes them with his sleeve.

> "Peace, perfect peace, with sorrow surging round?
> In Jesus' presence nought but calm is found.
>
> Peace, perfect peace, with loved ones far away?
> In Jesus' keeping we are safe, and they.
>
> Peace, perfect peace, our future all unknown?
> Jesus we know, and He is on the throne."
>
>
> Edward Henry Bickersteth

All the children have gone. Billy stays a little longer, trying to savour that feeling, not wanting to go to bed where he is afraid of his own dreams. Miss Stafford busies herself, tidying away her hymn books into the piano stool. She turns and notices that Billy is still there, and peers at him over her glasses sternly.

"What are you sniveling for? Go and get a handkerchief this minute."

Billy gets up slowly, his legs heavy. He leaves the hall with a heart so heavy, that he knows it is going to burst. He makes his way around the outside of the hall building and sits with his back against the wall. Here he is out of bounds. He folds his arms, puts his head on his knees and allows himself to cry. He sobs until he has no energy left, and "All in" is called.

Miss Brotherton is not at breakfast the next morning, so no one pays any attention to Billy's empty seat. He has gone to his secret place amongst the rafters in the roof of the classroom block. He pulls out his note book and forbidden biro and starts to write:

> Dear Mummy and Daddy,
>
> Where are you...?

His cloud has come down like a thick depressing fog. It surrounds him, penetrating his young mind. He cries softly until the bell goes again, and then tries to remember where he should be.

The first activity after breakfast is always P.E. or gardening. Billy is in no doubt about which he likes best. Jonnie and Mike have already arrived. Mike is struggling manfully up the slope from a small stream with a bucket full of crystal clear water which he pours carefully into the little channel carefully zig-zagging from the top to the bottom of a four by eight foot plot. The long thin triangles, outlined by the channel are each planted with a different crop. Lettuce, carrots, parsnips, spinach and around the outside, radishes.

Jonnie crouches, froggy style by the plot, carefully examining the rich brown soil for signs of life. He looks up to see Billy, hands in pockets, head down, trudging up the hill.

"Billy, look at this! The radishes are coming up!" The miracle of new life springing from the tiny black seeds is usually enough to make Billy's day, but nothing will lift Billy's cloud. Nothing will disperse the fog in his worried mind. He doesn't even stoop to look.

"You alright?" Jonnie looks up, concerned.

Billy sits on the grass, his feet pulled up, his head on his knees. He sighs. "Yes, it's just that I don't know what's happened to mum and dad. I hope they're okay. I haven't had any letters at all this term, and nor has Charlie." His voice begins to break, so he buries his face in his lap, not wanting anyone to see.

Jonnie sits beside him. He doesn't know what to say.

"Everything seems to be fine at Kasaji. I'm sure my mum and dad would have told me if there were any problems." He tries to be reassuring.

"But why have your letters got through from the Congo, and ours haven't?"

Jonnie has no answer.

Chapter 17

"The Widow Douglas she took me for her son, and allowed she would sivilize me; but it was rough living in the house all the time, considering how dismal regular and decent the widow was in all her ways; and so when I couldn't stand it no longer I lit out."

Billy finds it hard to understand why the words in Huckleberry Finn are put into such a strange order, and yet the book is being held up as a shining example of English literature. He is quite sure that if he muddled up his words like this Miss Brotherton would have no hesitation in making her feelings felt by warming up her shoe on Billy's posterior.

He hates the very word "Comprehension". It sounds like some new kind of punishment. He hates it because he knows that he will probably miss his morning break laboriously writing out the answers to the questions Miss Brotherton has prepared in an attempt to trap him into making a mistake.

Miss Brotherton sits, her legs crossed in front of the class, her shoe swinging menacingly on the raised foot. She reads slowly and intensely with an angry glower on her face between shooting piercing glances at her captive audience. Nobody dares do anything but sit up straight and look at her. Billy does not mean to be defiant, but the constant nagging worry about his parents has become a constant distraction. His mind wanders away. He stares out of the window, daydreaming, but not for long.

"Billy Walker! Are you listening to me?"

"Yes Miss Brotherton."

"Then what was the last sentence I read?" She glares at him, already shaking with rage. Billy turns pale. There is an uncomfortable pause.

"I, I don't know Miss Brotherton." She already has her shoe off.

She pushes Billy to bend him over a little further, Billy has forgotten to put his precious biro back with his note book, It is in his back pocket.

"What's this?" screeches the furious teacher. "You know Biros are not allowed in my class."

"I wasn't using it Miss Brotherton". Billy is crying.

"How dare you answer me back!" On the word "dare" the first blow makes a stinging slap on the back of Billy's legs, followed by more strokes than he can count. When she is finished he stands shaking in front of her. Miss Brotherton throws the pen on the floor and stamps on it with her other shoe until there is nothing left but broken shards of plastic.

"Now stop crying like a baby, and pay attention." Billy's leg and buttocks throb for the rest of the lesson as he tries to concentrate on answering the questions chalked up for the class on the blackboard. His hand is shaking so much that he has to use both to steady his pen. The bell goes for break time and he is only starting on the third out of five questions. By the end of break, he is still trying to finish his work, terrified at the thought of making mistakes. Miss Brotherton returns to set up for a French lesson, and is surprised to see him still hunched over his work.

"You need to go to your next class now, Come back and finish your comprehension this evening in free time." Billy gathers up his books and hurries away to his next class.

He has not eaten or drunk anything today.

Billy spends his day away from all his friends, and especially from Charlie. He knows the children will be talking about the beating, describing word for word what Miss Brotherton had said, how angry she was, and how many times she has beaten him. The humiliation is almost as painful as the colourful wheals that are beginning to show on his leg just below his shorts. He cannot sit comfortably so he lies in the darkness of the loft wishing the day away. He no longer has a pen to write down how he feels in his notebook.

In the darkness, Billy loses all sense of time, and for a while he falls asleep, exhausted from hunger and the trauma of the day. When he wakes, he listens out for the gong which will tell him that it is time for supper, but supper has come and gone without him. He is surprised to hear "All in" being called, and when he clambers down the shelves into the store room, it is getting dark. He hurries across the playground towards the boy's dorm trying to catch up with the others where he will not stand out, but midway across, he hears Miss Brotherton's voice above the chatter of the children, calling his name.

"Billy Walker, come here," she calls, while striding towards him.

Billy stops dead and turns towards her. As he does so, he realises that he has not finished his comprehension work. "She's going to kill me!" he whispers to himself.

"Have you finished your work from this morning?" She is short, but she still manages to tower over Billy.

"Yes, Miss Brotherton," he lies. Billy has never been a good liar.

"Then take me and show me!"

Billy was banking on her waiting until tomorrow to see his work. He knows that he is trapped. He runs ahead of his teacher who is already working herself into a new rage. Billy tries desperately to think of a way out, something he can do or say that will avert the coming wrath, but his exercise book tells the bare truth. The last question remains unanswered.

"You lied to me!" she screams. Her face a mixture of fury and satisfaction. "Bend over!" Billy cries out this time unable to clench his teeth and remain silent. The new beating is more severe than the first, and is falling on already painful bruises. "Don't you dare go up to the dormitory until every word is finished! After breakfast tomorrow you can go and see Mr. Birch, and we will see what he has to say about lying!" It is nearly dark before he can even pick up his pencil, and then he strains to see the page and finish his work. His writing is wobbly and untidy. He tries to imagine how Miss Brotherton will react to it tomorrow.

His work finished at last, Billy sits for a few minutes on the concrete floor, his back against the wall to compose himself, and to find the energy to walk out onto the playground. His little mind is spinning, and he falls asleep, exhausted.

Stiff and sore, Billy wakes to find that it is dark. He pulls himself up, shivering and tries to work out where he is. It all comes flooding back to him. He moves back to his desk, his head in his hands trying to work out what to do. By now the dormitory block will be locked. He can't bear the thought of trying to climb in and being caught. Every muscle hurts from the beatings of the day, and from lying on the concrete floor. The thought of facing the anger of Mr. Birch for lying brings tears welling up. With no one watching Billy lets them roll down his face. He longs for that long hug from his mum that always makes him feel safe, and then he wonders how his mum and dad are, and why no post has arrived. He cannot remember a time when he has felt so desperately miserable, and he can't think of anyone who he can talk to.

The decision is not a sudden one, to Billy it is not a decision, but more of a realisation. He cannot stay here any longer. He cannot face trying to meet the expectations of his teachers whilst he is so worried about his family. Somehow he must find his parents.

He is glad to be wearing his green pullover. The night air is cold, and the stars shine brilliantly in a moonless sky as Billy slips out of the school grounds and makes his way up towards the airstrip on the road that leads to Mutshatsha. He feels a mixture of fear and excitement, but the fear of staying and facing more punishment is greater. A dog barks as he makes his way into the silver starlight bathing the airstrip. Billy stops. He has left behind the one possession he really treasures. He wonders how he will manage without his butterfly net, but it is wedged behind his suitcase, out of reach. Reluctantly he abandons the thought of going back for it.

A bush fire has burned back head-high grass on the far side of the airstrip so that the road sign at the junction that Billy usually only sees on Sunday evening lorry rides is now standing high above the surrounding bush. Billy stands under it gazing up at it. The sign is white, and the letters have been carefully painted in black.

"Mutshatsha," he says out loud wistfully. He reaches up and strokes the post lovingly, as if carrying the name of his home puts it on his side. It is showing him the way home, and surely it can't be too far away. Billy turns left and begins to walk. He wonders how long it will take. In truth, he has no idea how momentous a path he is taking, or of the dangers that lie around and ahead of him. All he knows is that he cannot go back.

Chapter 18

The road is no more than an overgrown track with long grass growing down the middle, effectively creating two parallel paths to walk on. After a mile or so, the road forks. Suddenly Billy realises that he does not really know the way. He stands for a long time looking both ways, wondering which road to take. Eventually he goes right, sensing that the Congolese border lies that way. The fear of being caught and returned to school where he feels that punishment after punishment is being stored up for him, drives him on. He walks briskly, sometimes breaking into a trot. The path lies straight and definite ahead of him, and then he stops.

Three hundred yards ahead of him, in the starlight, something is moving, it has a rhythmic step, and Billy is now sure that it is coming towards him. His heart is beating fast, wondering whether to stand completely still, or whether to get off the path. Billy can hear his own breathing, and the cool air condenses his breath into a little cloud every time he exhales. He can see that an animal the size of a large dog is moving in his direction, and it appears to be dragging something. He stays still, and the animal keeps coming. Its head is low with sleek powerful shoulders. At forty yards it stops. Holding its ground, and holding its prey. For long moments they stare at each other, not daring to move, but each wanting to make progress.

Billy can see that it is a cheetah. It is too thin and long limbed to be a leopard, and he knows that lions do not live in this part of Zambia any more. It has a small antelope by the neck, still floppy, a recent kill that has not had time to stiffen up. Billy is not afraid. Cheetahs pose no threat to people, but he has never seen one this close up. They are usually very illusive, and do their hunting during the day. Determined not to lose its meal, the cheetah takes a few steps forwards and then crouches. Its eyes do not leave Billy's for a moment. Its meal rests safely between its front legs. Its whiskers move upwards as it hisses, and then growls softly. The little boy moves off the road to give way, standing quietly by a tree, and the cheetah continues on his journey. Billy can see now that he has a distinct limp, and appears to have a swollen hind leg. The little antelope is a duiker. His big "Bambi" eyes are wide open bringing a pang of sadness to Billy, but then he remembers how delicious duiker meat tastes once King George has roasted it.

Now Billy's path is marked out by big cat paw marks, and the trail made by the duiker being dragged. Here and there drops of dark blood, black in the early light of dawn confirm the route taken by the cheetah. It makes Billy feel he has a travelling companion, and then the cat's trail disappears into the bush off to the right and is gone. Billy is on his own again.

By the time the first shafts of sunlight are squinting through the trees ahead, the track is running steadily downhill. The two paths are now stony and deeply grooved, like empty stream beds, eroded by wet season rains, and for the first time Billy feels tired. He has been looking out for any signs that the route he has taken is familiar to him, but there have been no villages or notable landmarks. Ahead, there is the distinctive ribbon of thick "etu" forest which shows Billy that there is a river. He knows that he will recognise the bridge over the Zambezi, and the little missionary holiday cottage beside it. His legs are heavy, but the prospect of confirming that he is on the right route spurs him to a trot.

There is a corner just before the river where the road sweeps around to the right to meet it, but as Billy runs round the corner, his heart sinks. The road runs up to the edge of the river, and comes to an end. In the river there are two drums filled with concrete standing tall. The bridge itself has long since disappeared. There is no familiar cottage on the far bank. Billy sits on the bank of the river in the early sun. He is tired, and now he realises he is lost. He tells himself to be brave. He sits and thinks, letting his imagination take him back along the road he has taken. There is only one possible explanation. He should have taken the left fork and not the right.

A large rock sits at the top of a small gravelly beach at the side of the fast flowing river. The early morning sun is already warming it as Billy takes up residence on its flat top, to take stock of his situation. He is too tired to think straight, and his seat still aches from the beatings he has left behind. Somehow, though he feels safer, and more at peace here on his own, lost in the African bush, than he does at school. The only thing that really grabs his attention is his hunger. For the first time in days, he is desperate for something to eat. The gravel turns to sand as it runs down into the clear brown water in front of him. The sand makes a light background for a shoal of small fish that dart and play in the current.

"If only I had my net!" Billy says it out loud, startling himself, and then looks around to make sure no one has heard him.

The fish are out of reach. Billy gets up and looks around him for something, anything he can eat.

He remembers how his father's prayers for food were answered with the arrival of a real live goat, the day before the missionaries arrived.

Somehow Billy feels that his dad is better at praying, more likely to be answered. But he is very hungry, so he gives it a try.

"Please God, I need something to eat." he says, his eyes still open, looking around to see what, if anything, God will do.

The trees along the river are thick and luxurious. A bare branch sticks out like a bony finger over the river. A kingfisher sits, motionless on its very end, staring into the water and then dives. In a split second it is back on its perch, a shining, silver fish wriggling in its beak.

"It's alright for you!" says Billy, aloud. Somehow he feels comforted by the sound of his own voice, as if he is with a friend. Then he looks more carefully at the tree. It has thick, waxy, dark green leaves, brown and velvety underneath. Billy recognises it. There is one the same behind the sickbay at school. He knows that it is not an African tree, and he knows that the one at school has wonderful fruit on it. The fruit is so sought after that it is considered worth the risk of a good beating to steal quietly out of bounds to pick some. He had shared some secretly with Jonnie after lights-out only a few days ago in the comparative safety of the boy's washroom.

Forgetting his weariness, Billy clambers quickly up the river bank and disappears into the cool, dark shade of the Loquat tree.

Once underneath the canopy Billy gazes up into the branches. They are festooned with plump orange fruit. He gasps at the sight of them and pulls one off, stuffing it into his mouth. He has never tasted anything so delicious in his whole life! The soft white juicy flesh has a sweet, slightly peachy taste. Soon Billy's stomach is full, and the ground is dotted with the black seeds that have been spat out.

Seventeen years earlier, a newly married couple stayed at the missionary cottage. They sat on the bridge eating a picnic lunch, playfully taking it in turns to spit out their loquat pips, each aiming at a log lying in the river below them. Little did they know that one of those seeds would provide the answer to their own little boy's prayer many years later.

The kingfisher is back on his perch, still gazing intently into the water. Billy pulls off his green cardigan and rolls it up, taking a moment to press it against his face with a long breath to smell that distinctive smell of his precious mum. Using it as a pillow he curls up in the shade of the tree, and quickly falls asleep.

Chapter 19

He wakes slowly, the air is warm and full of the rich scent of the dry season. The river makes gentle gurgling noises where a rock nearly breaks the surface, and long bright green weed, trails in the current behind it like mermaid hair. He sits and looks around, letting his surroundings remind him of his circumstances. He has to decide what to do.

Behind him is the long track that provided his path last night. He thinks about retracing his steps all the way back to the fork where he went wrong, but he knows that this will take him close to school. If misspelling "February" is worthy of a whack, he tries to imagine the punishment for running away from school. A cold shiver runs down his spine, and he makes himself a promise.

"Don't worry," he says to himself. "I will not go back there!" So he rules out any thought of going back to the fork. This only leaves him with one option, and that is to press on. The river is too wide, swift and deep to cross without a bridge, and Billy feels that he should be further downstream, if he is going to find the point where the Mutshatsha road crosses the Zambezi river. The path seems clear to Billy. He will follow the faint footpath he can see running parallel with the river on the dry side of the "etu". First he kneels on the gravelly beach and splashes his face. He uses his hands to scoop water to his mouth. It tastes good, and he hopes it will not make him sick.

The afternoon is hot, and the bush is very quiet as Billy walks. He can hear himself breathing. The path turns out to be a well-used track, but there is no one walking on it at this time of the day. He can see the etu continuing on his right, reassuring him that the river is not far away.

By evening, his feet are sore and he is hungry again. With the sun still a little above the trees off to his left, he sees something that propels his tired legs into a trot. A bridge! It looks different, being approached from the river bank, and Billy is not at all sure if it is the one he is familiar with. To make certain he clambers up onto the road, looking warily left and right to make sure he will not be seen, but the road is deserted.

Now he is sure. The cottage is just on the other side, friendly and familiar. He runs across and is surprised to find tears welling up. This time they are tears of relief.

He is curious about finding the door ajar. It is usually locked. He pushes it open and is about to walk in, when he sees a padlock lying twisted and distorted on the ground. Now he feels nervous.

He pushes the door gently. It creeks a little as it swings open.

"Hello, is there anybody there?" He waits holding his breath. The silence gets louder. He is in two minds as to whether he should go in or stay out under the stars, but he knows that there is a bed in the cottage and it is getting dark. There might even be some food, so he edges in slowly. The room is empty.

The cottage has two rooms. One is a living room with an old wicker sofa and two rickety arm chairs. There is a plain wooden table with four wooden chairs. Some candle stubs lie on the table. The other room has a bunk bed and two single beds. The windows are covered with wire mesh and mosquito netting. There is no glass. Outside there is a small hut used for cooking and an old rusty barbeque.

Billy senses that there is something wrong. There are cigarette ends on the floor and a smell that he knows, but cannot place. It is part oily and part smoky, but it is not the smell of an oil lamp or a bush fire. It is not even the smell of King George burning the cooking. Then he remembers. His uncle Terry has a cabinet where he keeps his hunting rifles. It is the same smell as his guns. This makes Billy even more uneasy. He tiptoes towards the bedroom door, and calls out again.

"Is anybody here?" There is no reply and Billy soon realises that he is on his own.

Despite his anxiety, Billy still feels hungry. He opens the cupboard in the kitchen, and there amongst some packets of soup is a single can of baked beans. It is the most beautiful can Billy can ever remember seeing. He takes it reverently from the shelf and looks at it, wondering how he will open it. A quick search reveals only some plastic cutlery, so he takes the can outside into the gathering gloom and lays it on a flat rock by the river. By the door there is a rough stone that is used for propping the door open when it gets hot. Billy bashes the side of the can with the rock until a jagged hole appears. With a stick, he prizes the hole open until he can get a spoon in. The first spoonful is full of bits of dirt and wood from the rock and the stick. Billy is too hungry to care.

"You have to eat a peck of dirt before you die", he mumbles as he lifts the food to his mouth. He is used to hearing his granny say this, but has never been sure exactly how much a "peck" is, or whether this means that when the peck has been consumed your fate is sealed! Either way, the cold beans taste delicious, and soon Billy is asleep again, this time curled up on a real bed.

Uneasy dreams rise and fade in Billy's mind. None of them are coherent. Dark shadows move from tree to tree. Sinister faces appear for a split second and then disappear. Flames flicker. People crouch. Even in his sleep a new cloud thickens over Billy, gripping him with fear until he wakes up with a start and is surprised to find he is covered in sweat even though the night is now cool.

For the first time since leaving school, Billy feels frightened. The enormity of what he has done begins to close in on him. He lies in the dark staring wide eyed, his heart racing. He feels alone, lost.

"What if Mum and Dad are not at Mutshatsha?" he thinks to himself. "And anyway, I don't really know the way home, or how far it is!" "And who has been staying here? What is that smell?" The same questions go round and round in his mind, refusing to go away, and refusing to be answered. He lies awake for hours, until the first light of dawn begins to chase his demons away and he begins to fall asleep again. But then he is awake again with a start!

Bang, bang, bang!

The noise is so sudden and so loud, that Billy literally jumps off the bed. Then, bang, bang, bang, again, this time a little further away. There is a village only about a mile beyond the cottage, still twenty miles before the border with Congo. Billy can hear the sound of first one vehicle and then another start up somewhere near the cottage and more bangs, then in the distance the sound of shouting and screaming. He hides, shaking behind the door, but the noises seem to be getting further away, as if they are moving towards the village. After about five minutes Billy notices something new. Stars still shine in the sky he can see through the window facing the village, but the sky has turned orange, and soon there is the smell of smoke drifting on the breeze. Billy picks up his cardigan and a plastic bottle he has filled with river water. He grabs some packets of soup off the shelf and stuffs them into his shorts pocket. Then he slips out of the cottage. He no longer feels safe there. He runs to a clump of banana trees and hides amongst the thick leaves, wondering what to do next. A dog runs away from the village, over the bridge and on into the darkness. Billy can see that it is dragging one of its legs.

After a long time, everything is quiet. Too quiet. The new day slowly drags a reluctant sunrise into the eastern sky, and Billy begins to pick his way out of the banana plantation. Large brown crackly dead leaves make it impossible for him to move quietly, and now that an ominous silence has settled on the world each movement Billy makes sounds frighteningly loud to him. He stands in the open, in the clearing between the house and the trees. He holds his breath and listens carefully, but the world remains silent. The warming air is still full of the smell of smoke, a strange smell for this time in the morning. He is fairly sure something terrible has happened in the village up ahead. He feels pulled in two directions. Part wanting to make his way quickly away from the village and back towards school, and part desperately wanting to press on. This will take him into the village. He remembers seeing Kalemba from the car. The smouldering huts, and the charred remains of the dog are etched vividly in his memory, but the thought of going back is not an option to Billy, so he brushes off the dust and dead leaf debris from his clothes and creeps into a crude gulley running along the edge of the road. Leaning out he can see almost to where the village begins. The road is clear, but he decides to make his way along the gulley, not wanting to risk being seen.

Progress is slow, but now the smell of petrol mixes into the scent cocktail, and soon the remains of the first hut comes into view between the trees. Billy crawls up onto the verge on his belly, concealed in long grass. It looks like the whole village has been destroyed. The only building still standing is a little mud-brick church, but its thatched roof has been burned and there are shapes lying in the doorway. It takes Billy a few moments to realise the truth about these. There are four bodies in the doorway, and just outside a fifth. Billy can see it is a little boy. He is not moving, and flies are already swarming around him. There is a gust of wind which blows up a cloud of fine white ash, and a wooden roof support collapses into the interior of the hut nearest to Billy with a crash that makes his heart pound. For a few seconds he lies face down, trying to make sense of what has happened, then he begins to wriggle back into the ditch. He has seen enough. He lies there a little longer, giving himself time to think. He decides to make his way further into the bush so that he can find his way by walking parallel to the road where he can stay hidden, but as he begins to crawl away from the road he stops completely still. He is sure he has heard something. Yes there it is again! It must be a dog. The sound is not very loud, just a whimper. His curiosity, and a sense that it might be injured pulls at him. Still crawling cautiously, he makes his way back to the edge of the road opposite the village. He lies flat on his stomach and listens. First there is nothing but the crackle of fires still burning, then the sound again. The whimper. This time Billy's heart beats faster. He is not so sure that it is a dog. It sounds more like a person, perhaps a child. He cannot bear the thought of anyone still being alive amongst such devastation. He does not know if he can deal with the horror of someone lying injured and suffering. He holds his breath and listens. There is quiet and then the sound again. Now he is sure. A child is crying, quietly and without much strength, but the sound is unmistakable. Billy snakes a little further forward to get a clearer view. In front of him lies the whole horrific panorama; huts still smouldering, small fires still burning, bodies scattered around making grotesque, uncomfortable shapes, and the four piled up in the entrance to the church. The smoke is drifting towards Billy like a barbecue. For a few moments it strikes Billy that there is the smell of cooked meat, and then he realises to his horror that it must be the smell of burning people, He chokes on the smoke and buries his head in his arm, but now he can clearly hear the sound of someone crying softly. He is afraid of getting up in case the attackers are still around, waiting to shoot at anything that moves, so he scans the scene as bravely as he can. The nearest body lies with its head towards Billy. One leg is tucked under it, and the other lies out straight, Its head is tipped back and its eyes are wide, as if they are looking at him. Its posture has left the mouth open. A large dark patch of blood darkens the sand beneath it. Billy hyperventilates. Trying to stay calm his eyes are drawn to the bodies heaped together in the church entrance. He is sure that he has seen some movement there. He stares at the bodies. Yes, there it is again. A leg, smaller than the others, moves at the bottom of the pile, as if its owner is trying to get out. The crying seems to be coming from that direction too. Billy knows what he must do, but he is paralysed with fear. His face remains resolute, but tears well up and roll down his dirty face onto the sand. He wipes them away and then with all the courage he can muster, he gets up. Stooping, he runs across the road towards the pile of bodies, jumping over the little boy. When he gets there he is confronted by a confusing tangle of limbs and bodies. There are still flames burning inside the chapel. The bodies are covered in blood, but now Billy can see that there is a girl, about his own age, trapped at the bottom of the pile, She is trying to free herself, but the heat and exertion along with an injury have sapped her strength, and there is nearly no life left in her. Billy glances up to check that he is not being challenged, and then he grabs the arm of the body on the top of the pile and rolls it to one side. It is a woman. She grunts as the air is exhaled from her lungs sending a cold shiver through Billy. His hands are covered in her blood. Next there is an old man with a white beard. His eyes are closed. He is lying face up. Billy tries to pull him out of the doorway. He is surprised at how heavy he is, but slowly he drags him, inch by inch onto open ground. Lastly, there is another women, She is dressed in a blue, white and orange dress. She looks peaceful, but one side of her dress is soaked in blood. While Billy is still wondering how to move her, the girl finally manages to free herself. She sits up, and looks at the face of the women lying dead at Billy's feet. Then she throws herself on top of the lifeless body, screaming with new found energy:

"Mama, mama, mama!" For a few moments she is hysterical.

Billy shakes as he stands over the scene that has unfolded in front of him. He crouches beside the girl and lightly puts his hand on her shoulder as she cries. After a few moments she turns to him, and almost without looking, she throws her arms around him still sobbing, For a long time they sit side by side on the bloody sand, locked together in an embrace of sheer terror. The girl's whole body wracked with sobs. Billy is crying too.

Exhaustion saps the girl's strength so that she is no longer able to cry. Her body still tightens with involuntary spasms of grief, but even they are becoming less frequent, and less intense.

Billy still feels frightened and exposed. He gets up and takes the girl's hand, pulling her away from the village towards the bush, but she is determined not to leave the body of her mother. "No…" she says weakly as Billy pulls at her. She is still holding her mother's hand.

"We have to go!" says Billy urgently, looking around again. The girl looses the grip of her mother's bloodied hand and it slips away from her. She gets up and begins to run with Billy, still looking back at the body. They make it to the ditch and then clamber up the other side and away into the bush.

As soon as Billy feels safe, hidden amongst the undergrowth, they collapse onto the ground again. The girl lies, almost lifeless. Billy sits cross-legged in front of her, crying gently. He doesn't know what to do. She is wounded. Her dark blue top has a large black stain close to the bottom on her left side. She is lying on her right side, barely breathing. He reaches out his hand, still shaking and takes hers, a little gesture of comfort, and holds it as he tries desperately to clear his mind and decide what needs to be done. He can see her lips are cracked and dry from the heat of the fire, so he pulls out the bottle of water and tries to unscrew the cap. He has to concentrate to make his shaking hands succeed in this simple task, and then he holds the bottle to her lips and allows the water to trickle gently onto them. Without opening her eyes, her mouth opens enough to let a little in and she begins to drink. Billy has his cardigan tied firmly around his waist. He unties it, rolls it and then lifts her head gently to make a pillow. Within moments she is asleep. Billy watches carefully to see that she is still breathing. He is relieved that she is not in any obvious pain, and she looks peaceful for the time being.

Leaning back against the foot of a tree, he pulls his knees up so that he can rest his chin on them, and tries to think. His mind is full of a jumble of vivid pictures, most of which he wishes were not there. A little boy should not have to process that much horror. All the time he watches over the girl sleeping at his feet. Her rhythmic breathing is a little deeper now, and it begins to bring order back to Billy's thinking. He becomes aware that he is no longer on his own. For better or for worse, he has a companion. She will need looking after if she is going to get better, but this thought brings a strange kind of comfort to Billy. The loneliness and fear of being on his own, since being at the cottage, has been stressful, as if God himself has found the horror too gruesome to look at. Now he has someone else to worry about. He closes his eyes and begins to pray, the prayer of a little boy in desperate need of his daddy.

There is still a strong sense of threat in the air, and the smell of burning. Billy decides to explore the area around him to make sure there is no sign of danger, before planning his next move. The day is hot, and the sound of grasshoppers fills the air with their shrill discordant rasping, like amplified tinnitus. The surrounding bush is empty, though, and this helps Billy to feel a little safer. He drinks most of his remaining water, and then pours the last few drops onto his hands, washing away the blood that has dried there. Then he sits against his tree again, feeling much more able to think. The girl is still sleeping. Billy decides he will let her sleep as long as she needs to; at least until the evening brings cooler conditions. His pocket is still bulging with soup sachets. He pulls one out. "Cream of Tomato".

There are three things Billy needs if he is going to make soup. Water, fire and a pan. He knows he can get these from the cottage, but that would mean leaving his patient, and he is determined not to do that, so he creeps back to the edge of the bush, crouches in the long grass and scans the village. Fire will not be a problem. There is still plenty of burning wood around. Next to the remains of the closest hut there is a tall hollowed out log standing on its end with a stout pole sticking out of it. Next to it is a large plastic bucket. Billy cannot see inside it. Under what is left of the collapsed roof there are some blackened pans. From his lookout point he works out what to do. After glancing around he runs quickly and finds, to his relief, that the bucket is half full of water, but the pan he grabs is hot and he lets out a little cry of pain as he lets go. Quickly he picks up a piece of green banana leaf and uses this like an oven glove to pull out the pan. Then with the bucket in the other hand he runs back to the bush. His second trip yields two smouldering poles which quickly make the foundations of a crackling fire. Billy knows that making smoke and trying to hide are two incompatible activities, but since there is so much smoke going up from the village already, he does not think that a little extra will alert anyone to his presence.

By midday the girl's eyes have opened and she is asking for water. She tries to sit up, but finds that her side is painful when she moves, so Billy helps her, propping her against his tree. She sips some water, and then tentatively pulls up her top enough to examine her side. She has a gash about three inches long, still oozing blood, where a bullet has nicked her.

"At least there is no bullet inside you". Billy is surprised by his own voice. He has not spoken to anyone other than himself, since running away from school.

She looks up at him, her face stilled stained with tears. Her eyes full of anxiety. Fresh tears begin to flow. Billy crouches in front of her and takes both her hands.

"It's going to be alright", he says, trying to be reassuring.

The soup has boiled and cooled a little so that Billy can hold it up for her to sip. For a long time she cradles the pan with both hands and sips the soup loudly. Billy looks on, feeling pleased that he has been able to provide this simple comfort for her.

"What's your name?" Billy desperately hopes that she can speak some English.

"My name is Ruby." She says clearly. "What is your name?" Billy is so relieved to find they can talk to each other that he begins to laugh. For a minute they are both laughing, not really knowing why.

Another scout around the village has rewarded Billy with some groundnuts and some pawpaws, and Ruby has enough strength to stand. She has a strip of Billy's shirt tied around her waist to cover her wound which has been washed, albeit in rather sooty water. They spend the afternoon sitting cross-legged, and talking. Ruby describes between tears the horrors of the previous night.

"Who would do this?" asks Ruby waving her arm towards the village. "We are just ordinary people!" There is no answer.

"We can't stay here, it's not safe", says Billy, but the truth is he wants to get away from the death and chaos of the village as soon as possible, to be in a more peaceful place.

"I don't want to leave my mama", says Ruby, beginning to cry again.

"Ruby, she's gone", Billy looks into her eyes. There is so much pain. "We should bury her, but then we must go."

The ground is hard and unyielding, and Billy is surprised at how tired he is after digging for only a few minutes. He has found a hoe, and breaks up the soil which Ruby is pushing away with a flattened piece of wood. After about an hour a shallow grave has been dug, and the two of them stand there silently trying to catch their breath. They know that the next bit is the hardest. Billy takes Ruby's hand and gently begins to walk her back to the doorway of the chapel, but as the bodies come into view, Ruby loses her strength and crouches in the dust.

"No!" she cries, as if hoping that she will not find her mother dead.

Billy leaves her there and approaches the bodies that he had moved earlier. For a moment or two he kneels beside Ruby's mum, as if to check it is the right body, and to regain his resolve. Her eyes are closed. She looks peaceful, but when Billy takes her arm to drag her towards the grave he is shocked to find that the body has stiffened up. Eventually she is lying in the grave, still holding the same pose. Billy goes back to where she finds Ruby frozen to the spot. He takes her hand and tries to get her to stand, but she won't move.

"No!" she cries again.

"Ruby, you need to say goodbye", he says, choking back his own tears.

Slowly, falteringly, she makes her way to the side of the grave and stands there pitifully. The two of them gaze down at the body.

Billy feels that he needs to say something, but he has never been to a funeral before, and he does not know what to say, so the two of them just stand there holding hands. Tears are words enough, their grief, a kind of prayer, and a gentle, invisible calmness settles over them both like a blanket.

Then with Ruby still crying softly Billy drags the soil back over the body until it has disappeared. Ruby tears off a small piece of cloth from her skirt and lays it on the grave above her mother's head, and then holding tightly to Billy's hand, they walk back into the bush together, finally leaving the village behind them.

Billy wakes to find Ruby sitting up, looking at him. Her face vulnerable and scared. Half asleep, he reaches out his hand and takes hers, trying to be reassuring.

"Where are we going?" she asks anxiously.

This question refocuses Billy's mind on his own quest, so he sits up and looks intently at Ruby, thinking, but not speaking. The events of the previous twenty four hours have distracted him, even blurred his quest. For a few moments he can't remember what he is doing, but it doesn't take him long to find that yearning to be with his parents again, to see them and to know that they are alright.

"I've run away from school". Billy looks at the ground, a little ashamed. "I'm trying to get home to Mutshatsha. I haven't heard from my parents since the beginning of term, and with all the soldiers and trouble, I'm worried about them."

This is the first time Billy has actually verbalised his concerns for a long time, and putting them into words opens a window for Billy's own emotions. He is surprised to find tears are not far away. There is a lump in his throat. This time Ruby holds out her hand to offer comfort.

"I want to come with you. I have nowhere else to go."

A stream offers refreshing water, some fruit from the "etu" and a chance for Ruby to wash the wound on her side. It has stopped bleeding and is beginning to dry up. Billy is entranced for a few moments by the confetti cloud of butterflies that flutter and flicker in the pools of sunlight over the stream, and land, quivering ecstatically on the little sandbar that makes a miniature beach. They are almost all white with metallic purple tips, some are yellow and orange, but one is Kingfisher blue. It flies in fast and strong, settling on the sandbar to drink the briny water right at the edge of the sand. It opens its wings in slow motion, to reveal its full brilliant metallic colour. Ruby begins to get up, but Billy catches her arm, his face filled with awe and sits her down again.

"What is it?" she asks, looking perplexed.

"There", whispers Billy, without shifting his gaze. "The blue butterfly. Too beautiful to catch, too beautiful to kill." And then it is gone.

Whilst Billy is putting his shoes back on, a bird call stops them both in their tracks. Both children know that call, and their hunger instinctively makes them pay attention.

"Tala, tala, tala"; the call is frantic, and it is not hard to see a thrush-sized bird literally hopping from branch to branch on a tree leaning out over the river. It has a dark head and an unremarkable underside, but its tail is fanned out to make it more visible. "Peep, peep, peep!" Now it sounds like an excited blackbird. Billy grabs his water bottle in one hand, and Ruby with the other hand. He watches intently as the bird loops off into the bush, only to land on another tree about a hundred yards away.

"It's the honey guide bird." whispers Ruby. Billy already knows. The bird waits until his followers are nearly under its tree before flying on to a new perch, calling loudly all the way, Billy and Ruby follow for about a mile and a half, until they reach an old tree, barely alive. Its trunk is hollowed out and there is only one healthy branch left. The bird shuffles and fidgets on this branch, surrounded by an increasingly angry cloud of African bees, infamous for their aggressive behaviour. The followers stop and crouch at a safe distance. They have to weigh their options. Inside that tree there is fresh, rich African honey. But getting it will be dangerous, and there may be a price to pay for breakfast.

"We need lots of smoke", says Billy, looking intently at a dark hole about six feet up the wizened trunk of the dying tree.

"What will we put the honey in?". It soon becomes clear to the children, that despite the honey guide's expectations of a rapid response, this adventure is going to have to be carefully planned. They will need their precious pan, and the matches, so they retrace their steps back to the river noting the route. All the time, the honey guide hops angrily after them, this time following them. She scolds them impatiently.

"Alright, give us a chance!" says Billy. You will get your breakfast if you can just wait.

The children are energised by the challenge that confronts them, even excited. Ruby, holding Billy's hand tightly even skips a little, but then the pain in her side reminds her to move more cautiously. Back at the river, they find a place to leave the items they do not need, and they cover them in dry grass and leaves. They sit on the sandy strip that fringes the stream and plan their assault on the bee colony. Billy has seen King George do this before.

"We have to get lots of smoke into the hive, without getting too close. We can tie some sticks together to make a long handle with grass stuffed into the end. That should do it. Then I will climb up and get the honeycomb while they are all dozy. We need to get back as soon as we can. The bees will get more active as the day gets hotter." The plan is simple, straightforward, but the expression on Ruby's face shows that it is by no means going to be easy, or danger free. The bird still scolds them from the tree from where it first introduced itself, as if scorning their lack of boldness.

Billy is glad to have the matches from the cottage. Dry grass soon kindles crackling twigs with larger branches broken into burnable pieces added to build up the fire. Meanwhile Ruby uses the strip of cloth which has been acting as a makeshift bandage around her waist to tie some longer sticks together to make a six foot long smoking tool. A mixture of green and dead grass is them stuffed between the sticks at one end. The bird has stopped calling, and now watches from the live branch, its head tilted to one side, as if satisfied with the progress being made. Billy holds the smoking tool with both hands, rehearsing its use, working up the courage to use it. The morning has become warm and the deep drone of the bees moving purposefully in and out of the dark hole has grown noticeably louder.

First Billy looks at the tree and realises that he will have to use one hand to climb. There is a crack in the trunk that will give him hand and foot holes, and a dead branch about four feet from the ground will give him a useful place to stand while he attempts to smoke the bees out of their home. Billy's main concern is that the branch is a little too close to the entrance. He will have to move out on the branch to put some distance between him and the angry bees. Suddenly, he feels hopelessly underdressed. He puts the smoking tool down and puts on his cardigan for a little extra protection. Then he takes a deep breath and plunges the grassy end of the smoking tool into the flames. There is an immediate reaction. The grass fizzles and crackles, sending up a dense plume of sickly white smoke. The honey guide, excited by this development begins to "peep" loudly, and flies off its branch, deftly catching two bees as they fly out. After a few more seconds to make sure the grassy ball has reached its greatest potential for producing smoke, Billy strides towards the tree, trailing a thick stream of smoke and begins to climb. The bees have become agitated and fly around the entrance to their hive angrily, whilst the bird maintains a full-blown attack, darting in and out agilely picking off bees in full flight. Ruby holds the pan hopefully.

Billy is a good climber, and is soon sitting astride the branch near the hive. He holds one arm in front of his face, ducking as angry bees buzz around his face. He shuffles back along the branch until he is positioned about four feet from the hole and then maneuvers his smoking tool round so that the smoke from the grass is right in front of the entrance to the hive. The smoke is drawn up and into the tree and wisps of it appear a little higher up, escaping from cracks in the hollow trunk. For long moments the bees seem to become more agitated and active, as if the smoke is not working, Billy feels the intense burning of first one sting and then another on the back of his neck, but he is determined not to give in. The bird continues to encourage him with loud "peeps", but for every bee it catches, another hundred emerge from the hive. Billy covers his face completely with his arm, and then feels a bee crawling between his arm and his cheek. It stops and stings. The pain feels far more intense on his face, and makes him cry out!

"They are slowing down!" shouts Ruby, as if to encourage Billy to persevere. The smoke is blowing back into his eyes, making him cry, and although he cannot see what he is doing, he notices that the buzzing is quieter, and dares to peek over his arm towards the hive. More bees are crawling out, but not many are flying now. The honey guide is on the branch nearby, pecking at them. Now Billy feels as if he is prevailing.

"Yes!" he says triumphantly, still holding the smoking tool at the entrance to the hive. His cheek is swelling so that his left eye is half closed, but he shuffles forward a little to get the smoke a little deeper into the hive. After about five minutes Billy feels safe enough to crawl right up to the hole and he cautiously pulls out the smouldering tool. It has almost stopped producing smoke so he passes it down to Ruby. "I need more smoke!" Ruby drops the pan and quickly gathers more grass. In less than a minute, it is smoking with a new wad of crackling grass. Billy plunges it back into the hole, the smoke making tears which in turn make little gullies through the soot on his swollen face. After another two minutes, Billy passes the tool down to Ruby, and moves forward to peer down into the hole. For the first time he can see his prize; a large construction of honeycomb, dark brown and glistening with honey, about twelve inches down inside the tree. He pulls his cardigan sleeve over his hand and reaches in to break off as large a piece as he can take hold of. It comes away easily, oozing and dripping.

"Hold up the pan!" he shouts. Ruby is jumping up and down with excitement! The first piece of honeycomb drops heavily into the pan, and it is soon followed by enough pieces to fill it. Billy leaves the last piece on the branch for the honey guide. The bird is waiting impatiently. Billy drops the smoking tool and jumps down from the tree. For a few minutes Billy and Ruby dance round each other excited about their achievement, and then for a few delicious minutes they sit without talking, putting pieces of raw honeycomb into their mouths, eyes closed, luxuriating in its sweetness, spitting out the wax until they can eat no more. The honey guide joins the feast, pecking frantically at her portion, showering the children with small pieces of sticky honey comb. Billy can only see out of one eye, and his face is throbbing, but he feels as if he has won. He is enjoying being the patient now.

Ruby dabs water on his stings, and scolds him for getting honey all over his sleeve.

"Do you remember the story about the honey bird", she asks, like a nurse trying to distract her patient from his pain.

"Yes," says Billy, "but you can tell me". African stories are like a comfort rag to Billy. He has heard the full repertoire from Rhonda's grandfather. Better than going to the pictures, one of Billy's biggest treats has been to set off for the village during the holidays to sit under the mango tree and listen to one and sometimes two Lunda stories with all the drama and excitement an expert storyteller can convey.

Here, when the sun had set, the chores were over, and the fire was crackling, the whole village would meet and wait for the old man to come out of his hut. The children would clap and dance with anticipation and excitement, and the adults would fuss around them, settling them down to sit with the fire flickering on their faces. When it was completely quiet the old man would begin. Hours later, as Billy lay in his bed, he replayed the stories with all his own made-up pictures spinning through his head.

With the destruction of the village, all that has gone.

Ruby sits cross-legged in front of Billy, who is holding his soaked shirt tail against his throbbing eye. She sits up straight and takes a few moments to compose herself, and then the story begins:

"The bee and the honey-guide bird were very good friends. They would eat together, and talk together. They were very happy. But one day, Bee's mother became very sick. Bee tried everything he knew to make her well, but she was getting weaker and weaker. When he could do no more, he went to ask the advice of the witch-doctor!"

Ruby tries her best to look fierce, and uses a deep, gruff voice. "The witch doctor said: "you must ask your friend, Honey Guide, to give you a feather to fly. With this you will be able to heal your mother".

"So Bee went to find a child!" Ruby, still sitting cross-legged, leans forward and nearly whispers, "...because everyone knows a child is more reliable, and less likely to get bewitched and sidetracked, than an adult".

"The child went to Honey Guide, and said: "Your friend has sent me to you. His mother is very ill, and he thinks she will die. He needs one of your feathers to heal her." So the bird stretched out his wing and pulled out a feather. He gave it to the child, and told him to hurry back to Bee."

"Bee was very happy when he received the feather. He went, straight away to his mother and laid the feather on top of her. Very soon she was well enough to fly again, and Bee's friendship with Honey Guide became even stronger than before."

"Many days later, Bee found Honey Guide looking very miserable. "Why are you looking so sad?" said Bee. "My mother is very ill", said Honey Guide, "and I think she might die".

""Go to the witch-doctor, and ask his advice! He will know what to do," said Bee. So the Honey Guide flew off to see the witch-doctor."

Ruby uses her gruff voice again: "You must do the same thing your friend did for you. Ask Bee for a wing to fly. This will heal your mother."

"So Honey Guide went to find the child. The child went to Bee and said: "Your friend has sent me to you. His mother is very ill, and he thinks she will die. He needs one of your wings to heal her." Bee was very upset. "I can't give you one of my wings," he said sadly. "If I do, I won't be able to fly!"

"When the child returned to Honey Guide, she had nothing to give him. Things went from bad to worse for Honey Guide. His mother became more and more sick, until one day she died!" At this point, Ruby rolls onto her back, and lies flat out, leaving a dramatic pause in her story.

"Then what?" says Billy eagerly, though he has heard this story many times before. Ruby sits up and composes herself again.

"After that, Bee and Honey Guide never spoke to each other again. Their friendship was broken for ever. Honey Guide blamed Bee for the death of his mother, and he wanted to find a way to get revenge.

First he sang a sad song:

> "What Honey Bird saw on his journeys,
> Oh, what he saw.
> What Honey Bird saw on his journeys,
> Oh, what he saw.
> What Honey Bird saw on his journeys,

　　　　Oh, what he saw.
　　　　Mother is gone!
　　　　What Honey Bird saw on his journeys,
　　　　Oh, what he saw."

Then he thought about how he could get his own back on Bee. He was afraid to attack Bee because of his many brothers and sisters, so he learned how to talk to people, and to the honey badger. He called them to the tree where Bee and his family lived, and watched as Bee's home was destroyed. Revenge never dies by being put into practice, so Honey Guide became obsessed with destroying all the places where Bee's relatives lived. He will never stop calling the man and the honey badger! The end!"

Ruby sits up smiling. Billy claps appreciatively. "Come on let's go," he says. *(See appendix 1).*

Chapter 20

The children move through the bush away from the road. Progress is slow and their legs are scratched and bleeding, but they are afraid to use the highway. They do not know that they have slipped across the border, back into the Democratic Republic of Congo. No line has been drawn and no fence has been built. The local people live by the old ways. Their boundaries are between tribal areas. They care nothing for the lines drawn on maps on other far away continents. This is all Lunda land. So Billy and Ruby are mercifully spared the scene of death and destruction they would have seen had they used the road just a mile away. Here the border crossing has been decimated by Mike Hoare and his men. The barrier is twisted and broken, and the two guards, still in uniform lie dead; one man at the side of the road and the other a hundred yards further on where he has been dragged by the vehicle that hit him. The border office has been peppered with gunfire, and in a hut fifty yards from the road the body of a young man lies half-on and half-off a sleeping mat. A humbug tin has rolled across the floor spilling the last few sweets. The room is silent except for the buzz of flies.

The children are quiet; each living with their own thoughts. The elation of the previous day has evaporated. Billy feels anxious and upset. He feels a sense of urgency to move on, but knows that the great Mukulweji River lies ahead of them, with its crocodiles and swirling currents, a barrier that can only be crossed by the one bridge for two hundred miles in each direction. There they will have to take the risk of using the road, which will almost certainly be guarded. And what if the bridge has been destroyed again?

Ruby is feeling numb. The trauma of the attack on her village is weighing down on her, making her feel heavy. She keeps getting flashbacks which threaten to bring on attacks of panic. She tries hard not to think about what has happened, running up behind Billy and taking his hand.

The children have walked late into the afternoon before they eventually see the thick "etu" ahead of them; the sure sign of a river.

"At last" mutters Billy. Once in the etu there is a well-used path which snakes along close to the river. It is cool and dark, refreshing after the heat of the sun. There are glimpses of the river as it eddies and swirls along next to them. After twenty minutes Billy can see the bridge. He stops dead, squeezing Ruby's hand without realising it. There are some figures on the bridge, silhouetted against the late afternoon sky, but they turn out to be women walking back from the fields with big bundles of manioc on their heads. Billy is relieved to see them. These people are alive and going about their everyday business. But he notices that they are almost running, as if they are afraid, exposed. For a few minutes he and Ruby crouch in the shade of the etu, waiting for the ladies to move on. When it is quiet they move forward cautiously, until the old bridge looms up above them. It looks much bigger and more imposing from river level, but no more sturdy. The path slopes steeply up from the etu and meets the road about ten feet from the start of the bridge. When everything looks clear, Billy leads Ruby up the bank, She is shaking with fear, an overreaction in normal circumstances, but understandable in the light of recent events.

Halfway up the bank, Billy stops again, holding his breath and listening. At first he thinks he is mistaken. Perhaps it was the shrill sound of the grasshoppers singing their final rasping song of the day. But then, as he finds the courage to move forward, he is sure that there is another sound. The drone of an engine, a vehicle of some sort. Billy remembers the sound of the vehicles starting up near to the cottage on the night of the attack. His heart begins to pound and he turns and drags Ruby down the bank, slipping and falling as he goes. The children tumble and roll, coming to a stop just before the river.

There is no time to lose. The children both feel the rush of panic. Desperate to hide, and without thinking, they scramble under the bridge, into the space where it leaves the bank. The sound of a vehicle is louder now. It does not seem to slow down very much as it gets to the river, and soon it is clattering across the railway sleepers loudly. Terrified, the children cling to each other, their faces buried.

Chapter 21

Faith has not had much time to pack and flee the humanitarian disaster that is unfolding in Katanga. It has broken her heart to leave the hospital with a growing flood of casualties and refugees arriving every day. It seems so unfair to leave the African orderlies and nurses behind when she and John have a means of escape. But the children must come first.

John has come back from two days visiting villages and has heard more and more stories of the advancing mercenaries wiping out whole communities. He has decided to make the final decision to retreat into Zambia until the situation improves. They can use the time for a well-earned rest, and maybe even get a few days in the cottage by the Zambezi. He is worried about Faith. She is stressed and tired. She has not had any letters from the children, and wonders if hers are getting through to them. She feels detached and worried about them.

Granny, as stoic as ever seems to be taking it all in her stride, her knitting is beside her on the car seat, ready to go, should John decide that a stop is called for. So far, though he seems intent to get out of the Congo, and to Kalene in Zambia as fast as he can.

Up to this point John's greatest worry is that the bridge over the Mukulweji might have been blown up. Faith's relief when the old bridge looms out of the bush, unharmed is palpable. "Thank you God", she says, almost under her breath, and then she holds on to both sides of her seat as John hits the bridge, faster than usual, making the old sleepers rattle and clatter more than ever. In about fifteen seconds they are across. He pushes the reluctant gear stick into second, as the car begins to climb away up the hill towards the Zambian border.

Chapter 22

Billy can hear the sound of the engine change as it drops to second gear, and then slowly, to his relief, it fades into the distance. There is silence for almost a minute. He can hear Ruby breathing. She is still holding onto him. "You're squashing my hand", says Billy. They wriggle backwards out of the tiny space they have squeezed themselves into.

Stooping low, they half run across the rickety boards and on beyond the bridge until it is safe to jump across the ditch at the side of the road and into the cover of the bush again.

There is a great sense of relief that floods over them both as they take stock. "We made it", says Billy, emptying his pockets and then sitting on a fallen tree. "Let's make some soup!" He sits like a frog with his legs folded beside him stirring the soup as the fire crackles under the pot. Ruby comes back from a minor excursion with some fresh leaves that she throws into the pot to give extra flavour, and then the children both crouch, watching the leaves wilt into the little whirlpool of steaming soup.

"What happened to your father?" Billy asks, without looking up.

"He is gone."

"Do you mean he is dead too?"

"Yes, well I'm not really sure. Something happened to him." And then she stops talking, reticent to go on. But Billy wants to know. He looks up at her, trying to decide whether to drop the conversation or persist. Ruby is still staring at the soup.

"What happened?"

"First he was bitten by a dog, it jumped at him when he was carving some wood, and cut him badly on his face." She pauses, unsure about going on. "The dog had an evil spirit. It began to foam from its mouth and its eyes grew wide and angry, then it started to run around as if it was mad. The chief got his gun and shot it. The next day my father was feeling ill and the spiritman was called. He saw that it was because he had been bitten by the dog. He said the evil spirit from the dog had possessed him, and he said he must be thrown into the Mukulweji River. When he heard this, my Father tried to run away, but they caught him and tied him with ropes to his bed". Tears spring from Ruby's eyes again, and her young face grows old as she remembers. "They carried him away. He never came back home. I am not supposed to talk about him. If I mention his name, the evil spirit can come to me."

"When did this happen?"

"Before the end of the wet season."

"Sorry," says Billy thoughtfully. "Maybe you can come and live with us."

Journeys provide an intense seedbed for friendship to grow or break. Billy and Ruby become brother and sister, drawn together by the loss of their parents, though Billy is driven by the hope of being reunited with his, whilst Ruby, unsure of her future, mourns the loss of hers. Ruby is in the rare position of being an only child.

Her father, Kutela, had become a strong Christian and in keeping with his faith, had decided to marry only one wife. Katayi was beautiful with a bright outlook on life, and the only sadness she carried was that she was only able to bear her beloved Kutela, one child. Giving birth to Ruby had complications that nearly killed her, and left her unable to conceive again. Ruby has grown up in the special world of the only child, a true treasure. She has always loved her mum, who has done most of the practical parenting in the family, and on whom she has been so dependant, but she has adored her dad, with his smile and a sparkle in his eye, always ready to tell a story, and to sit Ruby on his knee. Losing her dad under such traumatic circumstances has been heartbreaking for Ruby. She still sees his face when the darkness of night surrounds her, in the twilight world between waking and sleeping. Her heart aches for him unbearably. Now her pain has been doubled by the loss of her mum. She feels numb, unable to think clearly. She cannot stop the horrific pictures searing her mind for brief instances, like flash photography in hell. She finds these wake her when she tries to sleep, and she snuggles up closer to Billy and looks for a hand to hold. Billy is always telling her not to squeeze so hard. Ruby dares not think about her past, and she cannot find any hope in the future. She can only live in the present, and as the next two days unfold, there is little to bring her comfort other than her friendship with Billy.

Billy's friendship with Ruby is deep and firm. He has felt lonely and worried for such a long time. He feels a deep sympathy, even an empathy with Ruby for the loss of her parents, and he tries to imagine what it must feel like for her. He loves the gentleness in her face, and yet he is finding that underneath there is a very determined young lady, older than she should be for her years. He shares a Christian upbringing with Ruby, albeit a very different one from hers.

Sitting together in the shade of a tree after the river crossing, Billy is thinking about the path ahead. "We should be able to get to Mutshatsha Mission in two days from here", says Billy determinedly. "We will keep of the road and try to get help from any villages we come to."

"Maybe all the villages are gone," says Ruby starkly.

With this thought nagging, they press on to the next village, which to their surprise seems to have been unaffected by the troubles. Neither Ruby nor Billy know anyone here, but the village is kind to them, feeding them their first proper meal for days. Billy cannot remember when chicken and nshima ever tasted so good. The children sleep soundly, somehow feeling safer amongst other people, though in truth this village is no less vulnerable and helpless in the face of the mercenaries than those that have already been destroyed.

The next morning dawns bright and misty. The early morning dew rests heavily on the jeweled grass after a cool night. Water and bananas set them up for their day's walk, and they have nshima wrapped in banana leaves to eat later.

"Look, a Ruby among the diamonds!" Billy says pointing at the dewy grass, laughing. Ruby chases him, as they leave the village. For a few moments they are children, happy and free.

Chapter 23

The railway line gives Billy hope. He knows that it will lead them in to Mutshatsha Gare. From there it is only eight miles to the mission station, and home! There are people at the Gare that Billy knows, Belgian officials that have hosted his family for dinners where Billy has had to put on his best manners, and Pedro's store, where he can get the world's most exotic and luxurious product; condensed milk! The children have strayed a little further from the road as their journey has gone on, so Billy is not sure how far they will have to walk, but at least he has found a straight and easy path with a definite destination. The children run down the track, trying to jump from one sleeper to the next, but soon tiring. The path along the edge of the track is well worn and travelers are frequent, walking in both directions. They pay little attention to the children though Billy is used to being stared at. There are very few white children in this part of Africa. At one point the tracks cross a stream, and the path turns sharply to follow the little waterway for half a mile to a place where a fallen tree makes a natural bridge. The children sit for a few minutes, their feet dangling in the heavenly cool water, until an old stooped lady with a huge bundle of sticks tied to her back wants to cross, and the children move on. Evening is falling as the children finally notice more shacks by the line, and Billy, to his delight, recognises the main road from Kolweji running close to the line.

"We are nearly there! Come on!" he shouts over his shoulder. Ruby is fit to drop. "Wait", she shouts as Billy begins to run. "Where are we going?"

"To Pedro's"

"Why?"

"You'll see," says Billy over his shoulder, still running.

Half a mile out, a train huffs and puffs up behind them, squealing and hissing as it wheezes its way into Mutshatsha Gare, heaving with passengers from as far away as Elisabethville and the Copper Belt. The children stop to watch as the train passes them at little more than running speed. Passengers are already jumping down beside the track, shortening their journey by not waiting for the station, and maybe avoiding the embarrassment of being asked to show a ticket!

"Come on," says Billy, "we can get a ride!" They run frantically, until the end of the nearest carriage is next to them. First Billy, then Ruby catch hold of the metal handrail and swing themselves up on to the bottom step leading up to the carriage door, narrowly missing an old man with a chicken who is trying to get off at the same time. The train loses speed and momentum as it chugs wearily into the station, and Billy knows just where to jump off before getting inconveniently trapped by the station.

Pedro's is literally across the road! There is the old familiar shop sign, but to his disappointment, Billy can see that it is already closed. Locked up for the night. He sticks his nose against the glass and gazes in at all the goodies; sauces and condiments, tinned food and blamanche packets, "Smash" mashed potato, even caramel Angel Delight! Billy feels as if he has been locked out of Heaven. And there on a shelf to one side, the thing he prizes most. A proud tin of Nestle Condensed Milk!

"Come on," shouts Billy again, running down a dirty alleyway to see if he can raise Pedro from his room at the back of the shop.

"You haven't got any money!" shouts Ruby.

Billy stops dead in his tracks, and then turns around looking pale. His hands fumble in his pockets as if hoping to miraculously find coins that he knows are not there. He stares helplessly at Ruby. He knows that when his mother shops at Pedro's she sometimes asks him to put the shopping on something mysterious, she calls "the tab".

"I'll ask him to put it on the tab", says Billy hopefully. By now he is at the back of the shop pounding on some crude bars that separate the interior of Pedro's from the rest of the world, and to Billy's delight out comes Pedro's ample belly, followed by the rest of him, his arms wide and a huge smile on his face.

"Billy, mon ami!" He engulfs Billy in a hug. "And who is zis beautiful young lady?"

"Ruby", he says beaming.

"Bonjour," he says, politely shaking her hand. "Come in, come in. You must eat!"

And so here they are, surrounded by Pedro, hungrily tucking into corned beef sandwiches and pickled onions. Pedro sits at the table. His smile has changed to a look of concern, as he looks at Billy. "I am surprised to see you still here," he says, his arms folded and resting on his belly. "Where are your parents?"

Billy keeps munching, trying in his own mind to predict how Pedro will react if he tells him the truth. He figures that he is too close to home for

Pedro to do anything other than to help him get back to Mutshatsha Mission, so he tells him the whole tale. Pedro's face remains implacable, but from time to time one of his bushy eyebrows goes up or a deep furrow appears across his forehead. At one point he gets up and disappears into the shop. "I am still listening", he shouts. Moments later he reappears with a tin of condensed milk and places it down on the table. Billy stops his story and smiles.

"I sink, if you were to tell me za trus, it is zis zat you want to see even more than Pedro! Non?" He gets out an old tin opener and makes two holes in the tin. One to suck the milk out and one to let air in. Then he makes another excursion into the shop to bring a can out for Ruby. Billy closes his eyes and savours the sticky sweet syrup. He almost feels that the whole adventure has been worthwhile. Pedro is sitting back at his place with his arms folded as if he has not moved, and Billy finishes his story.

Then Pedro looks at the children. Unmoving, he is obviously thinking, wondering how much to tell Billy.

After a few moments he says, "Your mother was in here three days ago. She was buying food for the journey. She said that your father was planning to go to Zambia as soon as he had finished visiting one of the villages."

Billy is so relieved to hear that Pedro has seen his mother, he does not pay attention to the rest of what Pedro has told him. "Was she alright?" he asks, trying to be brave, and wiping a tear from his eye with the back of a very grubby hand.

"She was fine, she was fine, zough maybe a little anxious. The sing is Billy, I am not sure if you will finds zem at the Mission. Maybe zey are already gone. Zere has been a lot of fighting and it is getting closer. I myself will be going to stay with my brozer in Kolwezi. I will be on tomorrow's train."

"But you have to help us", says Billy looking pale.

"Please", says Ruby imploringly.

"How can I refuse zis?" says Pedro, resigning himself with a sigh and a smile. "You must stay here. In za morning, we will go to ze mission in Pedro's lorry."

His attention has turned to the serious business of feeding the children proper food. To this end, he is tying a large bow in the back of a fresh apron which hangs off his ample midriff, making him look even larger than life. He uses a bread knife like a saw to hack off some doorsteps from a loaf of bread baked only that afternoon and then liberally coats each slice with margarine and Golden Syrup.

"You can't get by on condensed milk! Here is some proper food. You will sleep well after zis!" he says, proudly pushing two plates towards the children. The Golden Syrup is overflowing off the bread and making little pools on the plate. Billy's mum has always had a rather dim view of Golden Syrup: "Pure Sugar!" she says scornfully, and so she always scrapes it on very thinly whenever Billy persuades her, against her better judgment, to let him have some. So Billy relishes this much more generous approach to a spread that almost competes with condensed milk, for his affections! The meal is washed down with a glass of Coca-Cola, and the children are soon sleeping soundly.

Pedro's lorry is a well-known part of the local scene around Mutshatsha. Billy and Ruby are squashed into the cab with Pedro. Billy can hardly contain his excitement at finally getting home, but the excitement is mixed with a strong sense of anxiety. He wonders if his parents will be angry for the worry his absence will have caused. He wonders if they even know that he has run away, and he wonders if they are here or have already escaped across the border. He stares out of the window quietly. The tension increases as the noisy lorry grinds its way into view of the remains of Kalemba village. Not much has changed, though only a few scattered bones, picked clean, mark the spot where Billy remembers seeing the dead dog. He feels sad when he thinks about Divine and her family, but all that is soon forgotten as Pedro pumps at the clutch and finally grinds the gears into second with much French swearing, before the lorry clatters its way across the little river that Billy loves so much and begins its climb through the outskirts of the mission. The road runs straight and will bring the lorry up the drive to the Walker's house in less than a mile.

Ruby hears it first. The rhythmic drone that can only be an approaching single engine aircraft. At first it is hard to distinguish from the growl of the lorry's engine, but as it quickly gets louder, there can be no mistake. Billy, sitting by the passenger door, is looking east as the lorry heads north, so he sees it first. The truck is now directly in line with the end of the mission airstrip only half a mile to the west. There are two things that Billy notices about the plane as it heads directly towards them. The first is that it seems to be struggling to fly straight; the second is that the sound of the engine is irregular, surging and waning, and then coughing before going completely silent.

After that everything seems to happen in surreal slow motion. The nose of the plane rises, like a creature desperate for breath, then it comes almost to a complete stop, before stalling. The nose quickly pivots downwards, and the plane is diving straight at the lorry.

Pedro has sensed that something is wrong, but is still trying to drive.

"Stop. Let me out!" shouts Billy, and Ruby begins to scream.

The plane is silent for about three seconds as it falls, and then there is a huge explosion as it hits the ground twenty metres short of the truck. The force of the explosion blows the truck off the road. The world spins, there is light and dark, objects flying, crashing, splintering, screaming, burning, and then quiet. One wheel on the lorry, now on its side, spins for a few moments and then stops. Billy's head hurts. He is lying on top of Ruby, who is trying to wriggle her way upwards. They are both lying on top of Pedro, but he is not moving. There is blood, but Ruby does not know where it has come from. The window on Billy's side now faces the sky. The glass has gone. Panicking, Billy pushes his shoulders through the window. Smoke is beginning to fill the cab, belching past Billy as he climbs. By the time he is on the door, the smoke is thick and smells strongly of diesel. Billy reaches a shaking arm down into the smoke and immediately makes contact with another small hand searching furiously for something to pull herself up. They connect. Billy pulls as hard as he can, and bit by bit, Ruby emerges through the smoke. Now they are both huddled on the door, trying to take stock.

BANG! Another violent explosion sends them both spinning again. The fuel-tank on the lorry has gone! Billy finds himself lying on the ground, There is a loud ringing sound in his ears. His arm aches, there is too much dust and smoke to see anything. Disoriented he staggers to his feet and looks around. The lorry is engulfed in flames. He can't see Ruby.

"Ruby! Ruby!" he shouts more and more urgently, all the time staggering about amidst pieces of burning wreckage. Thick black smoke rises above roaring flames burning what is left of the plane which has broken into two distinct pieces. A column of acrid smoke also billows from the lorry. Then Billy remembers that Pedro is still inside the truck. He tries to walk towards the burning vehicle, but the heat overwhelms him, driving him back, so he carries on shouting for Ruby. He can feel panic rising, fearing for the worst, then he sees her. She is lying face down, her clothes burnt, in the ditch beyond the lorry, and dangerously close to the flames. Billy puts his arm across his face and darts in to grab her arm, dragging her backwards out of the ditch, up a small bank and onto some level ground in front of a corrugated iron house. There is yet another explosion. This time a tyre. It sends pieces of debris clattering against the house. Billy throws himself on the ground. He lies next to Ruby, who appears lifeless, their heads close together on the bare ground. Carefully he turns her head towards him. Her eyes are closed, her face grazed. "Ruby, wake up!" he cries. "Wake up!" She opens one eye and then closes it again.

"Thank God." says Billy, encouraged by this small sign of life. He still feels as if he is too close to the flames, and wonders when the next explosion will send more shrapnel flying his way, so he crawls backwards towards the door of the house behind him, and, still crouching, bangs as loudly as he can.

"Help!" he shouts, "Let me in! Help!", but no one comes.

Then Billy realises something he has not noticed up to now. There are no people around. No people at Kalemba, and that is understandable since the village has been destroyed, but there have not been any people this side of the river either, even before the plane crash. He stands up and casts his eye further afield, looking up and down the road, trying to see between the houses, but there is no one. It only takes a car to appear normally, and excited children swarm alongside cheering, a plane crash could be expected to draw a huge crowd. Where has everyone gone? And more to the point, why have they all gone? Something is wrong, something beyond this present crisis. Billy has a strong urge to run away and hide, but nothing will separate him from Ruby, who is still unconscious.

Billy tries to suppress the feeling of panic and clear his mind to decide what to do. He knows that Pedro is still inside the lorry, but he is sure that he could not be alive, and he is too frightened of what he might see if he looks. He decides that he must concentrate on getting Ruby to a safe place. The house next to them has a metal door which is secured by a padlock, but the next house has an open doorway with nothing but a beaded screen to separate inside from outside.

Ruby is moving a little and groaning. "We need to go!" Billy slowly gets her up onto her knees, where she has to rest, breathing heavily. "Come on, there might be another explosion!" He helps her to her feet, but she finds that one leg is too painful to carry any weight. Billy half carries, half drags her to the shack, and then inside, without knocking. The interior is dark and cool, and much quieter. There is a small table set under a window, with three chairs around it. Billy manages to get Ruby onto one of them, where she slumps over the table. There is a calabash full of water and a plastic bottle cut in half to make a jug. Ruby recovers a little more as she sips the cold water, shivering with fright. On another chair there is a pile of clothes, washed and neatly folded. Billy begins to go through them. Most are evidently adults' clothes but Billy finds some smaller ones that he thinks will fit Ruby.

"Try and get these on," he says, throwing them onto the table in front of Ruby "I'm going to have a look around."

The flames have not diminished, neither has the smoke, Billy remembers the village, and how he hoped not to see bodies! He does not look too closely at the lorry, where he knows Pedro will be, instead he wanders across the road to the gap between the houses where the plane has crashed. The main part of the fuselage is right in front of him, still burning vigorously. Billy's heart beats fast as he realises he can see the pilot, still strapped into his seat. His body is burned almost beyond recognition. The plane is still tilted so that the central section is pointing down at an angle, with the propeller bent. One blade has cut into the ground. The wheels are splayed out, and one has broken off. The passenger door is open and there is a second body half out, his legs still in the plane but his torso hanging towards the ground and one arm hanging down like a pendulum. Billy can see that from his hand hangs a small bag from a strap still wound round the body's wrist. It swings gently in the draught caused by the fire. Billy cannot get any closer because of the heat, so he makes his way around the other side of the house next to the burning plane. The house gives him some protection from the heat. Behind the house there is a yard marked off with barbed wire. Part of the fence has been flattened. Beyond the fence on open ground lie the remains of the tail of the plane, torn off but not burning. Billy notices three holdalls that seem to have spilled from the luggage compartment. One has split open, spilling clothes and toiletries. On the side of the bag is printed Cullinan Diamond Mine in pale blue letters. There is no sign of anyone alive, in fact there is still no sign of anyone at all.

Billy sits outside the shack where Ruby is resting, his back against a pile of firewood, knees tucked up under his chin, and arms folded around his legs. He watches, mesmerised as the flames on the burning plane start to die back at last. He jumps as a hand is placed lightly on his shoulder, and then looks up as he realises that it is Ruby. She offers him the makeshift jug full of surprisingly cool water. He drinks long and deep, and then pours some of the water over his head and hands, The day is hot enough even without the fire. Ruby has found an African dress. It has a black background and bright red and gold birds on it. Billy is pleased to see how much she likes it. Her leg is still hurting, but she manages to hop round in a complete circle to show off her new acquisition.

"I hope they don't mind", she says smiling.

"Who?" asks Billy.

"The person who owns the dress. Maybe, they'll come back."

The man half hanging out of the plane, his clothes still smouldering, suddenly drops out onto the ground with a thump which makes Billy and Ruby jump. It is almost as if he has come to life. For a moment they just stare at him, wondering if he will move again, but he lies still, in a disheveled heap. One hand is still attached to the little bag, which is now blackened and chard.

"What is he holding?" asks Ruby, tentatively edging a little further forward.

"I don't know." Now that the heat has died down, Billy finds he can move closer than before. The unburned edges of the bag are dark blue, it looks like it might be made of velvet. Billy can resist his curiosity no longer so he goes in search of a stick, and soon returns with a long piece of bamboo. He can just edge close enough to reach the bag which he prods with the small end of his goad. The bag is so badly burned that it disintegrates with Billy's first prod. The ashes fall away to reveal what looks like several glistening jewels, Unaffected by the fire, they glint and gleam in the sunlight.

Billy is lost for words. "Wow, look at that!" says Ruby. Her eyes have grown wide, and she edges a little closer. There is also a charred piece of paper which Billy quickly scrapes away from the bag to stop it from being completely consumed.

"What does it say? Ruby leans over Billy's shoulder as he studies it. The paper is burned on one side so that the right side of it is lost. It is headed with the words: Cullinan Dia...

"That's the same as the writing I saw on one of the bags", says Billy.

The left side of the paper has some typing:

    Mike Ho...
    Services Rende...

2.35 Carats
2.17 Carats
1.98 Carats
2.15 Carats
59.2 Carats: The Blue Butterfl...

Billy stuffs the paper into his pocket and turns his attention back to the remains of the bag, and the jewels. Carefully he uses the stick to clear more of the charred velvet away. As he does so Ruby gasps. Billy's efforts have exposed a pale blue diamond bigger than anything in his marble collection. It is dazzling, and Ruby cannot resist crawling forwards just close enough to reach out and grasp the stones. The children retreat back to the shack where Ruby rolls them out onto the table. There are five of them. Four are perfectly clear, round cut and flawless. They throw tiny pin-pricks of white light all around the inside of the shack, dancing on the walls and ceiling, but the children hardly notice them, for there among them is the one pale blue pear shaped stone that has taken their breath away.

Billy picks it up, turning it over in his fingers catching the reflection of the sky and letting it dazzle him.

"That piece of paper, it had a name on it!" Billy pulls it out and spreads it on the table. Now it makes sense. "This big one must be the Blue Butterfly!"

Even as he says it, Billy's mind goes back to the butterflies he has seen on his travels. He can see the flash of kingfisher blue so clearly in his imagination. He remembers how there was something almost magical, spiritual, about those experiences. He still does not understand why he was totally unable to even try to catch that blue butterfly, even though it would have made top place in his collection. It felt forbidden, as if catching it was going to desecrate something holy. Now here he is turning this amazing diamond in his fingers. When it catches the sun, the effect is just the same as the wings of that brilliant insect. Is it just coincidence that the diamond has that name?

As he turns it, the diamond seems to take on the same sense of being forbidden. Billy is not concerned about stealing the jewels. He and Ruby reason that they have been removed from a dead body. The person who owned the jewels is gone, that makes them fair game. But there is something much deeper going on; almost as if someone is speaking to him, warning him not to take it. Suddenly it feels to Billy that the stone he is turning is linked to some kind of evil. The blue flashes that keep dazzling him are sinister. Yet at the same time, the jewel is so beautiful, mesmerising.

Ruby hears it first. The faint, distant, throbbing drone of another plane. The children jump up, suddenly afraid again! Billy stuffs the diamonds into his pocket, and grabs Ruby by the arm.

"We must get to my house, it's not far, run!"

The sound of the plane gets louder. Its flight is steady as it passes over the airfield, and then makes its final approach to Mutshatsha Mission. The children reach the house as the plane touches down about a mile away.

Billy runs up the drive, anxiously. He jumps up the steps onto the veranda and into the house.

"Mum, Dad, it's me, Billy." No reply. Everything is quiet. Billy runs from room to room, but he knows they are gone.

"No, please no!" he cries. Mum, Dad, it's me, please be here!" He runs into the kitchen and then round the back of the house to Granny's bungalow, and bangs on the door. "Granny!" he shouts. "Granny". He bangs both fits against the door, over and over again, and then slides down, kneeling on the step where he can contain himself no more. He sobs uncontrollably. Ruby comes up behind him quietly. She puts both arms around him and lays her cheek against his back. There is nothing to say.

Then the door opens! There on the doorstep looking very bewildered is King George. He has Granny's stoutest walking stick in one hand, as if to protect himself, and when he sees Billy he goes in to a tirade of verbal sounds that conveys: "What on earth are you doing here?" and "You nearly sacred me out of my wits!" and then "Come here and give me a hug!"

Billy has never hugged anyone so hard as he hugs King George in this moment, but then he has never been so pleased to see him as he is in this moment. Their tears splash liberally onto Granny's step, and then King George looks up and sees Ruby. He puts Billy down and steps back to have a proper look and then with his arms wide open, questioning, he asks Billy with a series of actions, who the beautiful young lady is!

Billy picks up a stick and writes RUBY on the dry ground outside. He looks up and smiles. King George holds out a hand of greeting. They shake and then clap twice. Ruby does a little curtsey, to make sure the greeting is completed properly. Billy takes his stick and writes: "She is my new sister". That is enough for King George who welcomes them both inside, and insists that they sit down.

Billy looks anxious. He makes the familiar signs for "Mother and Father", and asks King George where they are. He replies with the sign for "over there" but adds a vocal sound which indicates that they are far away in another country. Then he picks up an invisible machine gun and begins shooting indiscriminately about the room. He indicates that this is something that is expected to happen soon. He moves to the window where the curtains are drawn, and looks outside furtively.

Billy is trying to take in all that he has learned. The mission is empty because an imminent attack is expected. King George, loyal to the last has refused to leave the Walker's house and is "dug in" with granny's walking stick as his only protection! Billy's precious mum and dad are as far away as ever, and he and Ruby are now in grave danger!

Chapter 24

Mike Hoare, and four of his most ruthless men have flown through the smoke of the crash site. Their rendezvous with the small plane from South Africa has not worked out as planned, and unless he can find the precious cargo being carried by that plane, he and his men will not get paid in diamonds as promised. He is relieved to see that the local population has got wind of his imminent arrival and have fled, leaving the mission and the surrounding area completely deserted. If he and his men can get to the crash site quickly, they can still retrieve the diamonds.

The door of the plane slides back and the commandos hit the runway before the aircraft stops. They head straight back down the airstrip towards the smoke rising half a mile beyond its end. Within ten minutes, they have arrived. After a brief pause to assess the situation, they see that there is no opposition and they run towards the smouldering fuselage. It does not take them long to find the remains of the bag, close to the charred body of the passenger. It does not take them long to realise that the jewels are missing, neither does it take long to work out that two small people, one barefoot, but apparently with a limp, and the other with European shoes, has been there since the crash.

The commandos swiftly and silently follow the footprints back to the shack, and then north along the road. The prints are not hard to follow.

Ruby is standing by the window, noticing how quiet and empty the world seems, when she catches some movement out of the corner of her eye, amongst some trees close to the house. She turns to look, but decides she is mistaken. Everything looks still. Then suddenly there is a loud bang as the door into Mum and Dad's deserted bedroom is kicked open just yards away. Billy and Ruby jump. King George does not hear it, but he feels it, and instantly he runs towards the children, catching them each by the arm, He walks them firmly to the door, and then opens it a crack to look out. The coast is clear, so he carries one of them under each arm the ten yards to the big hot water drum raised up over the fire place. Quickly he pushes first Billy, then Ruby on top of the drum and then climbs up himself. The drum is lying on its side and a crude hole has been cut with an acetylene torch big enough for them to get inside, one at a time. The drum is empty except for a residue of rusty water at the bottom, and it is almost impossible to move quietly, but within a few moments, they are all squeezed in, like fledglings in a nest.

The commandos are frustrated and angry. The trail has led them to the house, a careful check has confirmed this, but a painstaking search has revealed nothing. There is no sign of those distinctive prints leaving the property, and no way that they can see that the children could have left without leaving prints. After about an hour they settle down to eat, and then decide they must search a little further afield. Hoare sets off with two of the men towards the generator house and then the school. He sends the other two to search the hospital and church.

King George sees them go as he peers through a small hole at the top of one end of the drum. He knows he must get himself and the children away as soon as possible. He also knows that the commandos are following the children's trail, though he does not know why! He indicates silently to the children that they must not move, and then carefully he tiptoes back into Granny's cottage, re-emerging seconds later with a pair of her slippers, and her wellington boots. He puts them up onto the drum and tells the children to put them on, Then he beckons for them to jump down and they run across a small piece of open ground, under the guava tree past the chicken run and on into the bush. The pair of slippers are a luxury for Ruby who is used to going bare foot. Billy is not getting on well with Granny's boots. They are too big for him, and already he can feel a blister developing on his right heel. Once they are deeper into the bush, they sit for a few minutes on the side of an ant hill to catch their breath. Billy indicates that he wants to put his own shoes back on, but King George persuades him to go a little further in the boots. He tries to indicate that they must keep moving, and Billy asks where they are going. King George writes on the dusty ground with his finger: KALENE.

Kalene is where Charlie was born, only twenty miles away from the school, back in Zambia.

"If only we had been watching the road" he says to Ruby, "we would have seen them." And then he remembers the car crossing the Mukulweji bridge, and how they had hidden from it! One thing is clear. It is much too dangerous to head back towards Zambia using the road. King George knows the old routes through the bush, heading further west towards Angola, and then approaching Kalene from the opposite side. He figures that this will take them out of the area being terrorised by 5 Commando, who seem to be moving ever further north in their campaign of terror.

What he does not know is that the only thing that Mike Hoare is interested in right now is picking up the next installment of his wages, and those of his men. Everything else will stay on hold. After all, how hard can it be to liquidate a couple of kids?

King George leaves the children near to a small stream, then returns to Kabweba, his village to collect a few supplies, including an old backpack the Walkers have given him. Two hours later he is back, the sun is getting low, and King George is determined to put miles between the mission and their overnight stop. Billy slips off the boots and puts his own comfy shoes on again.

The path is only big enough for walkers, but it is a well-used route between Mutshatsha and Kayoyo where there is a bridge over the Mukulweji. King George does not feel comfortable using such an exposed route, especially as the route is deserted except for them, so he takes them on smaller paths, rarely used from one village to the next until they come to a place where a village has been long deserted. Here the sandy soil has run out of nutrients and the village has moved on to a new location where they have burned off some of the bush to grow crops and start again. The old village makes a good overnight refuge. One hut is still more or less intact, though populated with a noisy colony of bats that are just waking up for a night's hunting as the travellers arrive. One by one they stop chattering and drop off the blackened roof frame, flying off into the night, until the hut is quiet again. The children are tired, exhausted from a long and traumatic day, so they sleep as King George fetches wood and lights a cooking fire in another hut, trying to make as little smoke as possible. He has brought some sweet potatoes, and some dried fish which he breaks into a pot of soup.

The "work-harder" pigeon is calling up a new dawn as Billy gets up and goes out for his first toilet visit of the day. There is a clear spring of water coming straight out of the ground at the edge of the old village. Here they are close to the great watershed between that which will run off into the Zambezi and head south east towards the Indian Ocean, and that, only a few miles away which will run off into the Congo River and head North and then west, before flowing into the Atlantic. Billy loves the gentle sound of the tiny stream as it trickles over a root, making a miniature waterfall. He washes his face and hands and then ambles back to sit outside the hut until the others wake. He puts his hand into his pocket and pulls out the Blue Butterfly. For some reason, Billy has not made the connection between their pursuers and the stone in his hand. He pulls out the charred piece of paper and lays it on the log beside him, and then tries to work out which of the smaller gems matches each carat size listed. He uses the Blue Butterfly as a paper weight to stop the morning breeze from blowing it away.

King George emerges next, yawning much louder than he thinks! He looks first at Billy, then at the stones he is playing with. Then he reaches down and picks up the shimmering blue diamond. King George uses signs to ask Billy: "Where did you get this?" Billy mimes the plane crash and then acts out retrieving the stones from the wreckage. King George picks up the paper. Mike Hoare's name is known but never more than whispered by the Lunda people. King George's eyes grow wide as the situation becomes clear to him. He throws the stone on the ground, as if it is infected by a contagious disease, and then begins to shout and holler. Billy jumps up and puts his hand over his mouth to stop him from being heard a mile away! King George picks up the stones and quickly zips them into the side compartment on his rucksack, then he comes out and sits on the log next to Billy. Ruby has woken with all the commotion and is sitting with them too. King George can do nothing but shake his head. He does not know what to do. Now he knows that their pursuers will not give up until they have the gems, but he is also sure that Mike Hoare will want to know that anyone aware of their existence is terminated. Simply returning the jewels to him will not be enough. There is nothing for it but to get into Zambia as soon as possible and hope that he will not follow them all the way.

King George quickly works to get rid of any signs of their overnight stay. There are bananas and some ripe shindwas for breakfast and the travellers are on their way again. Their pace is even quicker than the day before and from time to time Billy has to trot up behind King George to slow him down, Ruby is still weary from days of walking, and her leg is bruised from the explosions and the lorry crash.

Late in the day, they reach the outskirts of Kayoyo, a small settlement, just big enough to be called a town, but too small to remain anonymous, so King George finds a safe place in the bush to rest and then goes off to try and find some food. He has nothing more than a wooden sling, some large ball bearings and a knife. Nearby he finds a watering hole, used by domestic animals in the day time. It is dark now, and deserted, but to his delight, King George sees that a large monitor lizard, some three feet long is taking advantage of the quieter conditions and has come out of the bush for a drink. The first shot with the sling hits the lizard with a dull thump, stunning it. King George runs up, kills it with a swift slash of his knife and dinner is secured.

Billy cannot remember eating monitor lizard before, but he trusts King George's taste in caterpillars, so it seems only logical to try out his lizard recommendation! King George uses his knife to construct a spit to which the lizard is attached whole. And then the fire is lit and it is only a matter of time before dinner is ready. After about an hour, the spit is carefully lifted off the forked sticks that are holding it and the lizard is laid on a smooth rock. King George gingerly pulls at a back leg, which comes away easily, and then cuts a strip of meat from the belly. Billy is surprised to find that it is satisfyingly meaty, although a little tough and stringy. Ruby is already asleep, aching and exhausted she is too tired to eat.

The evening air is still warm as the other travelers make themselves comfortable and fall asleep under a million African stars.

Chapter 25

His vest stained with body salt, and his tattooed arms deeply bronzed, an automatic rifle slung over his shoulder, he kneels and stares at the footprint in front of him. He has a broad South African accent.

"What do you see here boss?" Hoare ambles over to look.

"What are you thinking?"

"I'm trying to understand why anyone would want to wear rain boots in the middle of the dry season. And another thing; I am asking myself why these footprints show the gait of a child, even though the prints are adult sized, unless of course this is a child who doesn't want to be followed and is trying to fool us."

Hoare moves closer and looks at the series of three prints that lead away from the water tank. Then he looks more closely at the other prints. "They have an adult with them", he says slowly. "Looks like we have a trail to follow, let's go!"

The commandos move quickly from one clue to the next, and begin to pick up a sense of where their quarry is heading. Soon they find a pair of discarded wellington boots, and pick up the track for Billy's shoes again. They quicken their pace.

A scrawny cockerel does his best to announce the new day to his harem and the world in general. King George wakes, and Billy soon joins him. Ruby stirs, but she has a temperature, and does not want to rise. King George realises that they must rest for at least a few hours. Maybe they can set off again when the sun has passed its hottest in the afternoon, and walk into the first part of the night. There will be a good moon.

He indicates to Ruby that she should stay and get as much sleep and rest as she can, whilst he and Billy go into the township to get some supplies. It is market day in Kayoyo. The regular road side stalls have quadrupled in number. Batteries, and spinach, light bulbs and pineapples, monkeys and brightly coloured cloth, everything a man, or woman could possibly need is available for the right price. The road is thronged with locals and visitors from villages as far as fifteen miles away. Billy is fascinated by the ladies' hairdressing stall. There is a sign over the stall which reads: "Nicole's Hair While You Wait". Here one corpulent lady is sitting on a stool surrounded by no less than eight hairdressers, all dressed in grey two-piece costumes. Four of them are working on her head at the same time, combing and straightening her hair and then plaiting threads of hair into an intricate pattern. Even with four of them working, the lady is still there, and little progress has been made when King George, satisfied with his purchases, heads back to the resting spot up on the hillside, overlooking the town.

The combination of pineapple and a good rest has done Ruby good, and she is looking much brighter by the time King George decides to set off with Billy on his second expedition of the day. The only road in the town leads straight to the river, where a bridge crosses the Mukulweji, larger and stronger here. King George is concerned that the bridge constitutes a danger point for them. If anyone is following, they will know that there is little option for the travellers other than to cross the bridge. He approaches cautiously, keeping off the road. The bridge is open for all to see, with a steady flow of people coming and going from the market. King George does not like it. Crossing here will leave them too exposed, even if they cross at night. Down to the side of the bridge there is a little jetty built out into a calm part of the river. On the side closest to the bridge there is a place where women are washing clothes. Children splash excitedly nearby. On the other side there are some dugout canoes tied to the jetty or pulled up onto the bank. King George leads Billy down to the jetty, and indicates to him that they should hire a canoe. Now Billy has a chance to try out his Lunda, something that he is not allowed to do at school. After making initial enquiries, Billy finds out that one of the canoes is owned by a man who lives in a shack a hundred yards downstream. Half the building is constructed out over the river resting on stout wooden poles, and an elderly man with only one good eye is lounging in an old armchair on the decking looking out over the river. After polite greetings have been exchanged, followed by some fierce bartering where at one point Billy is accused of "wanting to drive an old man to his grave", and all the time King George flaps about like an injured bird making loud cries of dismay, a deal is finally agreed. There are warm handshakes and everyone is good friends again. King George swings the backpack onto the deck to find some money. First he puts his hand into the wrong side-pocket, and nearly pulls out one of the diamonds, before realising what he is doing! The old man explains to Billy that there is a crossing point a mile further downstream. They can leave the canoe on the far bank, and his brother will tow it back tomorrow.

Billy loves paddling, and he is getting strong. King George sits in the bow giving loud and unintelligible directions, as Billy pushes the canoe clear of the sandy bank and then jumps in to start paddling. The current is strong and the boat makes rapid progress to a place outside town where the etu is thick and a little gritty beach makes a landing place for their canoe. Two others are already beached and tied with rope bark to an overhanging branch. King George can see that this is a good place to fish, so he pulls out some line from his pack, Billy helps him to find some worms, and soon they are sitting in the back end of the canoe, King George holding the line lightly as it drifts downstream in the current. In half an hour they have caught five rather bony tilapia.

The river has taken them a little north of the town, but since the resting place is on the north side of the town, it is easy to find a path winding its way first through thick etu, then out onto the open hillside where they can see the spot where they left Ruby.

Billy runs ahead, excited about the canoe, and wanting to be with Ruby. It is he that finds that she has gone! At first he thinks that she must be nearby, finding a toilet spot or going for a little walk. He calls for her, but there is no response. Then King George arrives and throws the fish onto the flat rock that has become their dining table and work surface. There on the rock is a piece of folded paper with a stone on top of it. King George looks at it. The implications begin to sink in. He takes the paper and opens it slowly. Billy is standing with him.

It reads: "You have our rocks, we have your girl. If we don't get them back she will be dead before the sun sets. If you want to see her alive wait here and we will make an exchange with you."

King George knows enough English to understand the message. He grabs the fish and the pack, replaces the folded piece of paper under its stone, waves at Billy and they disappear into the long grass, frightened that the commandos are watching them. He crawls under a thorny bush with Billy and lies there panting, his mind racing. They cannot talk, but each is processing the situation. Waiting for the commandos to come back is not an option. Even if they bring Ruby, they are both sure that these men are so ruthless, that once they have the jewels they will not leave the travelers alive. Leaving Ruby to the mercy of these men is not an option either! The only thing they can do, is to try and turn the tables on them, to track them down and find a way to free Ruby before she is killed. King George knows that as long as they have the diamonds, they are worth more alive than dead! Both know what they must do, but neither has any idea how they are going to do it!

One of the commandos has a deep bite on his forearm. He is embarrassed and annoyed that such a wound should be inflicted by a little girl. He does not notice that he is leaving a trail of little blood droplets, and since he is at the back of the column, none of his comrades notice it either. Hoare is moody, angry. He has the girl, but he still does not have the stones. He can't believe that this simple exercise has now occupied him and his men for two days. He speaks to the man in front of him:

"Go back and watch the site. Don't let them out of your site. Shoot them both if you can, but make sure you get the stones first!"

By the time he gets back, Billy and King George have slipped away and are hiding under their bush.

The commando reaches the rest site and looks around quickly. He sees that the message is undisturbed and decides to lie in ambush for Billy and King George. They can just make him out through the long grass, and they can see the muzzle of his rifle sticking up behind his back. Then they hold their breath as the commando lies down on his belly, rifle in position. He begins to wriggle back into the long grass just ahead of them, so that his feet are coming closer to their hiding place. Billy prays that he will not look round and see them. His heart pounds and he nearly faints, but the mercenary is intent on watching the resting place and the rock.

Billy and King George are only about two yards away from the commando's feet, the heavy black soles of his combat boots seem to be looking at them! He settles down, prepared to wait as long as it takes. He slides the bolt on his rifle up, and then forward filling the chamber with a live round and slips the safety catch off. His finger rests on the trigger guard, ready to fire.

For over an hour, no one moves. Billy quietly places his face on his hands and prays that God will somehow give them a way out. King George dares not flinch. Moving silently is an art when you can hear, but when you are deaf it is almost impossible. He knows that one mistake will mean death for them both.

At last the soldier wriggles forward, gets up and quickly disappears into the thicker bushes on the other side of the clearing, apparently going to answer a call of nature. King George sees a window of opportunity and gently taps Billy on the shoulder, As quickly and silently as possible they begin to inch their way backwards down the slope, keeping the thorn bush between them and the rest area, and keeping their bellies on the ground. The further they go the more confidence they find, the faster they go until they are out of sight. Then they sit up and look at each other.

King George draws a map on the ground, a look of angry determination on his face. He draws the rest area showing the bush and the commando hiding in his place. He shows the path they have come on and he indicates that they are going to go back along the path in search of Ruby.

"What will we do when we find her?" writes Billy. King George picks up a stick lying beside him, lifts it above his head and brings it down on the ground with all his might and an aggressive yelp! Billy puts his hand over King George's mouth to stop him giving them away.

The sun has almost set. Stooping, two figures run across the slope keeping below the brow of the hill. Lights are coming on in the township below. When they are well beyond the rest area, they circle round to come out on the path that brought them here yesterday. King George studies the dusty path carefully, then stoops to look at a sticky drop of blood that has still not completely dried. He fears that it might be Ruby's but he is sure that if there is more it will provide a trail they can follow. After half a mile the military boot prints move off the path, and King George struggles to follow the tiny drops of blood in the fast vanishing light. The trail is only short. Under an acacia tree there are two tents. Silhouetted against the sky Billy can see the figure of one of the soldiers sitting on a log, his rifle resting on his knees. Tied to the tree he can see Ruby, her mouth gagged and her hands and feet bound. Bad as this is, he is relieved to see she is still alive.

The fading light is on their side. King George thinks about a course of action. The soldier gets up and uses some matches to start a fire. The wood is already built into a neat pyramid. There is no sign of the other three mercenaries, but there is no way of knowing if any of them are in a tent.

King George comes to the conclusion that there will never be a better time to free Ruby. The ground around is rocky and bare. It does not take him long to find a large rock that he can carry. He indicates to Billy that he should stay where he is, and disappears off to the left into the darkness. Billy waits for what seems to be an eternity. The soldier casually gets up and goes to check that Ruby has not loosened her bonds before ambling back to sit on his log, firelight dancing on his face and blinding him to the darkness around him. He has a pile of groundnuts that he is working his way through, and puts his rifle down to make the task a little easier. It is now quite dark, but a silver glow on the horizon promises a brilliant moon rise.

For a few more moments it is almost completely silent, then suddenly from out of the darkness King George appears. The rock raised above his head with both hands, he runs forward and with a blood-curdling scream he brings it down on the top of the commando's head. Dazed, he slumps forward and tries to reach for his gun, but King George gathers up the rock and swiftly deals him a second blow which renders him senseless! Buoyed on by King George's victory, Billy jumps out of his hiding place and runs forward to help. He hopes none of the other mercenaries have heard King George's war cry! King George has already got his knife out, and has cut Ruby free. Billy grabs the rifle, and they run down the hill together tripping and sprawling several times in their haste until they have covered about half a mile, and they feel a little safer. Their eyes are full of excitement. They cannot believe what they have just achieved, but they know that they have stirred up a hornet's nest!

The moon is rising above the trees on the far side of the river, turning the waterway into a silver ribbon running from south to north ahead of them. The township and the bridge can clearly be seen about a mile away to the left. King George calculates that their canoe must be almost straight ahead of them. Now a little more carefully they pick their way through the open scrub on the hillside and into the darkness of the etu. First they try working their way south along the river bank but Billy remembers an old tree with roots like a hundred snakes reaching down into the river. He had admired it earlier in the day from the river when they were paddling downstream.

"We must go the other way!" He turns and pulls King George by the arm. Valuable minutes have been lost, but soon they come out onto the gravelly beach. Here another dark shape has taken up residence for the night. A crocodile, almost as long as the dugout raises its head and hisses at them menacingly. Billy knows that on land the travelers are safe as long as they keep a respectful distance.

Four dark shapes move quickly and silently down the slope. The commandos are not used to being made to look foolish and Hoare's men cannot remember him looking so angry!

The canoe slides smoothly off the shingle and out into the river. Billy digs the paddle in and pulls with all his strength, again and again, angling the craft upstream to compensate for the current. The crocodile slides into the water at the same time, leaving nothing but its eyes showing above the water. The moon reflects from its retinas like the headlights of a distant car.

Then the quiet of the night is broken as automatic fire breaks out, and bullets kick up splashes all around the canoe.

"What are you doing, you idiot!" shouts Hoare. "If you sink the dugout, we will lose the stones! Get after them!" Two of the commandos slice through the bark rope holding beached canoes and soon there is a chase across the river. Billy is no match for the soldiers who are closing with every stroke. King George can see that they will get caught before they reach the far bank, but he is determined not to be boarded without a fight. Ten yards from the far side, one of the boats rams roughly into the escaping canoe. King George stands up and swings hard with the backpack, still half full of sweet potatoes. He misses and loses his balance, sending him plummeting into the black water, and causing the canoe to lurch and capsize, throwing both children in after him. Billy manages to grab the rifle, and does his best to hold it out of the river.

"Get the bag!" shouts Hoare, and one of his men dives into the water surfacing feet away from King George who is still gripping the pack with his right hand, whilst thrashing wildly with his left in an attempt to swim to the bank. The commando reaches him in one deft crawl stroke and places his hand on King George's head, pushing him under. Billy and Ruby are struggling to get to the bank. Billy feels the bottom of the river underfoot and pushes himself as hard as he can against the water. When it is a little shallower, he turns to reach out for Ruby, but now he can see that the commando is only feet away, and he has the backpack. King George is nowhere to be seen.

Then quite suddenly two things happen. King George rises to the surface spluttering and gasping, and the commando lets out a loud cry and disappears below the surface, only to reappear a second later with a look of terror on his face. Billy realises that the crocodile has the soldier's leg and is pulling him back into the river. The pack floats free again as the beast begins to corkscrew, forcing the soldier under the surface. He does not come up again.

Billy has grabbed the pack and he and Ruby run up the bank. King George is right behind them, still spluttering. The current has pushed the other two canoes a few yards downstream. Billy has never used a rifle before, but King George is a good hunter. The children are lying on the river bank, gasping for breath. King George crawls up the bank after them, still coughing. He reaches out and takes the gun from Billy, pointing it first one way and then the other, terrified that they will be caught at any moment.

This bank is shaded from the moon. It feels dark and sinister, noticeably colder than on the other side, as if the sun has not shone on this bank. The travelers hold their breath. The commandos must be only feet away,

There is nowhere for them to run now, nothing else they can do. There is just one rifle against three.

Then the shooting begins. A long volley of shots, and the sound of bullets hitting trees and ground, fizzing into the river and ricocheting loudly from iron roofing then more firing and some loud eerie screams, almost inhuman, like spirits in the night, and then for a few moments, silence. Not even the frogs are croaking. King George and the children lie shaking with fear, but there is no sound. Nothing is moving. They keep very still for a full half-hour, and then King George begins to snake his way up the bank a little further beckoning to the children to follow. Ahead there are some shacks. One has a door open, but as they approach, Billy trips and falls, and then jumps up frightened. There at his feet is a body, its face down, A beam of moonlight shines onto the lifeless head. King George comes up behind him cautiously and rolls the body over. The children jump back, and Ruby lets out a shriek! The face of the body is covered in a black and white mask, and has feathers along the top to make a head-dress. The body is bare-chested and looks dead, but the mask looks very much alive as if it is looking at them, or even through them! Even King George lets out a yelp, and pulls the children back as if the body offers some threat or contagion. The travellers give the corpse a wide berth and then creep into the shack. They carefully search the two rooms inside to make sure it is empty, then sit on the floor in one corner for a long time, watching the pool of moonlight on the floor moving slowly across the room until a restless sleep relieves them of their worries for a few hours.

Chapter 26

King George is the first to wake, and by the time the children are up and about he has been out to try and work out what has happened, and how safe they are. Billy asks King George who the dead man is, and King George, takes a stick and writes on the hard floor of the shack, a single word: SIMBA.

He takes Billy by the hand and leads him back towards the river. There, close to the water, lies another fallen commando. His throat has been cut. It seems that both sides lost a man in the skirmish.

Billy tries to ask King George how the Simba knew that the mercenaries would be here, but king George does not know. The travellers do not feel safe. There is a deep sense of anxiety in the air, as if they are being watched. The masked man does not look any less frightening now that it is light. They slip away quietly and are relieved when the warm sunlight welcomes them onto a path that leads away from the shack, first to the west and then takes a sharp turn between two manioc fields towards Kayoyo again. The manioc plants grow to about six feet in height and they have been planted on mounds like potato ridges. The travellers are completely hidden in here. They wind their way through the plants rather than on the path.

King George still has the pack, and Billy ponders the fact that yesterday morning they were being pursued by five elite commandos. Now as far as he can make out, there are just two left. But the threat has not gone away.

The travellers are not sure which route to take now. Hoare will expect them to stay on course, heading west. There is no point in pursuing the original circuitous route, now that he knows where they are, and must have worked out where they are heading. King George decides that it will be best instead to follow the river south, going upstream towards the bridge that the children had hidden under as the Walkers were driving over it. This will mean a complete change of direction, and might throw Hoare off their scent. It will bring them back to the road leading towards the school. Billy makes it very clear that he does not want to be returned there. He dare not think of what punishment might await him if he did! He writes: "I AM NOT GOING BACK TO SCHOOL" with his stick and makes King George shake hands solemnly to seal the promise.

The travellers are edgy and nervous. They know that Hoare will not stop hunting them until he has his precious gems. King George makes one last foray into the township, and comes back with two pairs of flip-flops, and a second-hand pair of shoes for himself. He figures that with new footwear and a path used by many people, young and old, they might become inconspicuous.

King George feels a little safer now that he is armed. The rifle is a Russian-made AK-47, and looks and smells like it has had a lot of use. It has been acquired with just one magazine, fully charged with 30 rounds. King George puts it to the semi-automatic setting, so that if he needs to use it he can make every precious round count. The local population think nothing of seeing members of the public carrying guns, so they do not look twice as he does his shopping.

The rest of the morning passes without incident. The path runs beside the river except where it meanders around a loop. At these points the path takes a short cut. My midday they have covered about ten miles, though with the path twisting around they are still less than halfway to the bridge. The day is exceptionally hot and still. The grasshoppers seem to relish the heat and increase the volume of their shrill rasping. The children need to rest and drink, so King George branches right towards the river which is about a quarter of a mile from them at this point. They push their way through head-high grass until they get to the bank of the river and the dry skeleton of a tree. A lazy fish eagle glides effortlessly off a branch over the river as they approach and skims the water before rising into the scorching sky. The travellers are inside the apex of a tight loop in the river. The current runs fast and deep on the far side, where it has undercut sandy cliffs. A kingfisher emerges from a hole in the sand and darts away downstream. The near side of the river is still and balmy. King George chooses a place where the river is well-shaded and then he draws out his line and hook, He has some leftovers from the monitor lizard, wrapped in some paper and growing smelly. He ties the line around a small stone, attaches some bait to the hook and lets it plop into a quiet pool under the tree. Ruby curls up in the shade and is asleep in minutes, but Billy watches the line intently. After about ten minutes it suddenly begins to move, making a little "V"-shaped ripple as it does so. King George stands up and pulls gently on the line, trying to assess whether he has something on his hook, or whether a wily fish is just making off with the bait. The line keeps moving so King George gives a quick jerk on the line. There is an immediate reaction. The line changes direction and starts moving much quicker. King George has the line tied to a stout stick. All the slack on the line has been fed out, so he begins to pull the fish in, bit by bit, winding the line around the stick until the fish makes its first appearance at the surface. It is a big mudfish with dark brown back, broad whiskered head, and golden belly. It thrashes and writhes like an eel, and all the time King George winds it in. Billy runs to help, taking the stick and line so that King George can paddle into the shallows with his knife to dispatch the fish. Egged on by success, King George goes back to fishing, and Billy goes back to watching.

Then something catches his attention; some movement across the river. At first he only sees it out of the corner of his eye, and when he glances up, he can see nothing, but then there is some movement, again. This time he can see that it is a camouflaged figure, in the shade under a tree. The man is stooping, his thumb in the strap of the rifle slung across his back, and with his other hand lifting water from the river to splash on his face. Billy freezes. King George is about to throw hook, line and sinker into the quiet part of the river again, but Billy manages to stop him by waving at him, and then pointing. King George sits perfectly still, hoping the shade of the tree will hide them. The commando gets up quickly and melts into the trees on the far bank. In seconds he has vanished.

Billy and King George stay still for a long time. Now they know that Hoare has worked out the route they are taking, but they also know that at least one of the mercenaries is on the opposite side of the river. They take their catch to a hidden spot and light a small fire to cook the mudfish. Billy has always loved the white tastiness of mudfish, and he is hungry. Ruby wakes for lunch, and the three of them sit together thoughtful whilst they eat.

King George decides that it is no longer prudent to follow the river up as far as the bridge. Hoare and the remaining mercenary will ambush them there. Somehow they must get across the river and strike away from it through the bush. About two miles behind them, the travelers had passed a village before stopping for lunch. Billy is sure that there must be some canoes there, so they decide to backtrack. It is mid-afternoon and the village dog makes a half-hearted attempt to challenge them as they approach. There is an old woman sitting outside a hut, her eyes clouded with cataracts. Billy greets her and asks to see the village headman, She says nothing but points to another hut across an open communal area at the centre of the village. Billy calls a welcome at the dark entrance and a voice inside calls him in. He goes through the whole ritual of making a proper welcome again, and then asks the old man if there is a canoe for hire. The old man looks at the little party, and clearly does not trust them to hire a canoe, so he tells them that if they want a canoe, they must buy one. The price comes to far more than the few coins that King George has left in the backpack, so frustrated they turn to leave. Then Billy remembers something and catches King George on his way out. Undoing the zip on the side of the pack, he reaches in and finds one small stone. Moments later the gem is sparkling in the palm of his hand. Billy decides to reopen negotiations, and soon a canoe has been bought with a perfectly cut, flawless, two carat diamond! A good deal, Billy thinks. After all, what use is a diamond?

The travellers lose no time in pulling their new acquisition down to the water's edge, and after a brief survey of the far bank they push off, digging the paddle that has come with the deal into the dark waters of the Mukulweji River. Ten minutes after being purchased, the canoe is abandoned on the far bank and the little party with backpack and AK-47 set off in a new direction for the second time that day.

Although there is no recognisable path, they make good progress. The bush is open and dry. King George keeps a good eye on the sun to maintain his sense of direction, and to calculate how long they have been walking. When the sun is about an hour from the horizon they find a sheltered spot to settle for the night. It is dark by the time the sweet potatoes are dragged out of the fire, and the weary travelers finally fall asleep feeling safer than they have for several nights.

King George wakes early. It is still dark. He nudges Billy and Ruby with his foot. Billy cannot understand why they are starting so early, until King George acts out the hunting and skinning of a duiker. The children stretch, drink some water, put on their extra layer of clothing, (it is cold and misty) and follow King George to the edge of a large open plain with a boggy area and a waterhole. He motions for the children to wait and then he creeps forward, the assault rifle ready. He is used to using a sling or the stealth of a bow and arrow, but he is quite excited about having a rifle to hand. First he crawls, then he snakes forward on his belly until his head comes out of the grass and he can see that there is a group of gazelle, and a bushbuck quite close. He does not want to shoot one of these, They are too big to carry, and he does not have the tools to butcher a larger animal.

A little further on, barely visible in the early morning mist, a duiker is silhouetted against a white background. It would be out of range for bow or sling, but King George adjusts the sights on the rifle to 200 yards, and aims carefully. He holds his breath and squeezes the trigger. The bang is so opposite to the silence of the morning, that it surprises King George as the gun kicks back against his shoulder. Hundreds of birds fly up in unison from the grass and the trees, rudely awakened from their overnight roosts. The gun shot echoes off the hills around, and the little antelope drops dead.

Billy hopes that Mike Hoare and his companion are a very long way away!

King George spends the next hour and a half carefully sharpening his hunting knife on a stone and then butchering the duiker. They will keep some to eat and sell some in the next village to generate some useful cash, thus preserving them from the need to squander any more of their diamonds!

The next village is far away from the beaten track. They are not used to seeing travellers of any sort and so the little white boy is an instant celebrity. A dozen children come out to giggle and stare shyly, until they find that Billy can speak Lunda. After that, they forget about the colour of his skin and treat him as a new playmate. He finds whatever he can to entertain them. It does not take long for King George to sell his excess meat, but no one in the village has any money so he bargains for some supplies. He gets some salt (always good to use as currency), some fruit, a tin of corned beef, a tin of powdered milk, two tins of baked beans with sausages, and some manioc flour. Lastly he acquires a big bunch of greens all tied up in a bundle with some string. King George now has all the ingredients for making Billy's favourite dinner. The travellers have been offered a hut where they can sleep tonight- a luxury after sleeping outside for so long. King George sits outside and takes his shoes off. He takes up position on a log with a cooking pot between his feet. His toes hold it fast as he begins to mix a little boiling water with some manioc flour and a pinch of precious salt. The process is slow and requires a fair amount of strength. When the mixture has reached the consistency of porridge, King George takes it off the fire and puts another pan of water on with, the greens, some chopped chilies a tomato and some herbs. This pot will make the "kuda natchu" or relish. Billy squats contentedly on the other side of the cooking fire slowly turning a large piece of duiker meat on a spit. King George still has the nshima pot wedged between his bare feet, but he is using some banana leaves as padding so as not to get burned. Slowly the flour and water merge into a heavy ball of dough. The meal is ready.

Ruby comes to join the dinner party. Each person uses their right hand to break off a piece of nshima about the size of a golf ball, and then they use their thumbs to make an indentation, thus turning the nshima into an edible spoon which can be dipped into the relish. The nshima with its little reservoir of sauce is then consumed. Pieces of duiker have been cut for each person. The meat is dark and rich like venison. Billy thinks he is in heaven. He would happily exchange any diamond for a meal like this! A circle of smiling, chattering children watch them eat until their mothers call them in for their own food.

Refreshed the travellers rise early to get on their way while the day is still cool, and plan to slip away unnoticed, but by the time King George emerges with his back pack and rifle looking like a wildlife ranger, the whole village is up and excited about seeing them off. They have exchanged most of the rest of their duiker meet for a live chicken that Billy is carrying in a raffia bag. Only its head is sticking out. The little children all want to hold Billy's hand, and even Ruby has become a celebrity, with flowers in her hair and a copper bracelet that one of the old ladies has given her. Billy is starting to feel that maybe the worst is behind them.

Chapter 27

Travelling is slower and more difficult today. The bush is denser, and on several occasions they have to turn back and find another way forward when the dense elephant grass becomes impenetrably thick. Then they come to a stream which is too deep to wade, so they walk along beside it until they come to a place where a tree has fallen across the stream to make a natural bridge. King George has grown tired of carrying the rifle, so the chicken which has now been named Snow-White, because of its white head, has been passed to Ruby, and the rifle is now being carried by Billy. He has always hated the idea of anything being killed, unless of course it is going to be eaten, and he feels uncomfortable carrying the gun over his shoulder. He is surprised at how heavy it is. It feels like an alien object as if it should not be with them, It is an intruder, but it has already supplied them with meat, and it might yet save their lives, so Billy settles for an uneasy truce. He tolerates it.

They balance across the fallen tree one by one. Billy notices that the stream is running south west. It must run into the Zambezi. He feels that the journey must be more than half completed, as if it is all downhill from here. Now there is a faint path for them to follow, but Billy hangs back to have a wee in among the thick trees by the stream.

Completely without warning the two commandos step out in front of King George and Ruby as they emerge from the etu, rifles raised, blocking their way forward. Ruby instinctively drops the chicken and raises her hands, terrified. King George freezes, there is nothing else for him to do.

"Take off the pack and put it on the ground!" Hoare's voice is deep and menacing.

King George does not hear him.

Don't fool around with me! Do it NOW!" shouts Hoare.

Ruby is crying. "He's deaf. He can't hear you. Please!"

Hoare uses the muzzle of his assault rifle to indicate that King George should hold both hands forward, then he walks up to him and strips the pack from his shoulders. He lays his rifle on the ground and begins to search the pack looking in the main compartment first and then unzipping the side compartments. He pulls out three small white stones and holds them for a few seconds, admiring them, before stuffing them in a pocket in his combat jacket, then he begins to search the rest of the bag. He looks up and shouts at King George again.

"Where are the other two!?" King George continues to stand still, his hands raised.

"Where are the other two!?" He shouts again, then he begins to search first King George, and then Ruby. "WHERE IS THE BLUE BUTTERFLY!" he bellows. King George looks bewildered. All the time the other soldier has his gun raised ready to use it.

"He faces up to King George, their noses touching. "I don't care if you are deaf, you have five seconds to hand over the other two stones or my friend McCann here will shoot the girl." As he says it the other soldier slips off the safety catch and loads his weapon.

"One, two, three, four, five! A single shot rings out. King George shuts his eyes, too frightened to look, but when he opens them, he sees McCann slumped across the path, and Billy standing about thirty yards away, his rifle smoking and pointed at Hoare.

"We don't have them," says Billy shakily.

Hoare doesn't know what to do. His rifle is lying on the ground more than ten feet away, and he has seen that Billy is not afraid to use his AK-47. His eyes move from Billy to his own rifle and then back to Billy. He stands and looks at him. "What do you mean, you don't have them? There were five stones!"

"I know," says Billy dryly, "but we spent one and lost the other."

"Spent one?"

"Yes, we hired a canoe with it." A look of incredulity comes over Hoare's face.

"Hired a canoe with a diamond worth thousands?"

"Thousands of what?" asks Billy.

"And where is the Blue Butterfly? He asks intently, still not daring to move.

"I dropped it." says Billy, blushing. I was playing with it at the village last night. The children wanted to see it, and I thought I put it back in my pocket, but it has gone."

Hoare looks at him through greedy slit eyes. "You think I'm going to believe that?!" he takes a step towards Billy.

"Don't! I'll shoot you, I really will!" The muzzle is shaking, but it is still pointing at Hoare's chest. The commando is sure that Billy has the blue diamond, and he is not going to be thwarted by a child, so he launches himself at Billy. Billy closes his eyes and pulls the trigger. The setting has slipped to fully automatic. A volley of six shots arcs up into the sky as the recoil knocks Billy, still holding firmly to the assault rifle, onto his back.

All six shots miss their target, Hoare is onto Billy in a flash, pinning him to the ground and drawing a combat knife from his belt. King George leaps into action, pulling his own knife and leaping on the back of the commando. They roll over, each fighting as if their life depends on it and Billy scrambles to his feet. In desperation he fumbles with the rifle again, trying to change the setting on it so that only one round gets fired at a time. At last he slips the lever to semi, and another shot rings out.

This time it is Ruby who is lying on her back, a smoking rifle by her side. Hoare lies still, face down, a dark red patch growing all the time on the sand around his head. King George untangles himself from the commando's body and sits on the ground to catch his breath. He looks at his arms and legs to make sure they are unharmed. Billy and Ruby throw themselves on him, rolling him over, laughing and crying at the same time. They are free! Five Commando is no more!

King George opens the pocket on Hoare's jacket and rolls out the three diamonds he had taken. Carefully he picks up his pack, along with some tins of supplies that have been thrown out and repacks it all into his backpack. Then he sits Billy down in front of him, his hands on Billy's shoulders. He looks him straight in the eye. He holds his fingers up as if he is holding the Blue Butterfly, and raises one eyebrow. Billy looks embarrassed again. He has never lied to King George, and he does not intend to now.

"It's true" he says, even though he knows King George can't hear him, "I had it just before we left the village, but I can't find it now. There is a hole in my pocket." He turns his pocket inside out to show an inch long tear in the seam.

King George shakes his head in exasperation and then gets up with a very loud sigh.

Chapter 28

Everything has changed. The anxiety of travelling with a constant feeling of threat has gone. There is no need to battle through the bush any more. The road across the border is only about ten miles east. No need to carry a rifle anymore, so with the chicken's dignity restored, and the backpack adjusted, the little party set off in high spirits, leaving the dead commandos and their tools of war behind them. Three days hard walking should bring them to Kalene. At last Billy feels there is real hope.

By evening they step out onto the road between Mutshatsha and the Zambian border. Ruby is quiet. She knows they will have to pass her village, bringing back memories of the attack. She is glad that the men who did it are all dead, and wonders how many other villages have been spared the same fate as hers. That night they sleep at another friendly village, and the chicken's life is prolonged when the travellers are fed by the locals. Ruby has a relative here who is thrilled to find her still alive, having had news of the destruction of her village. She takes Ruby under her wing and gives her some fresh clothes to wear. She tries to persuade Ruby to stay with her, to make a new home there, but something inside Ruby makes her want to go on. Her connection with Billy and King George is strong though they have only known each other for a short time. They have been through so much together.

So a little tearfully, she waves goodbye to her aunt the next morning and sets off into the unknown with her travelling companions.

Billy is still blissfully unaware of what has happened at the border crossing. Mercifully, the bodies have been removed and two local young men, seeing a self-made career opportunity, have set up as the new customs officials at the border. They have mended the barrier bar and have even "adopted" the uniforms of the previous employers. They are finding it quite lucrative, and so far it seems that no one in official office knows that the real customs officers are dead. It was no secret that the customs men, were supplementing their meager wage by asking for much more than they were supposed to. The new officials feel, that since they are not being paid by the government at all, they should increase the unofficial levy for crossing the border.

King George, the children and the chicken arrive in the middle part of the day, and do not intend disturbing the men in the customs shack as they are clearly enjoying a mid-day siesta. Only their feet can be seen, resting on the customer counter. Pedestrians are usually allowed to walk through without being accosted. It is normally only drivers and passengers in vehicles that are charged. King George lifts the barrier to let the children through, but it creaks loudly and wakes the customs men. They sit up with a start, and straighten their hats and uniforms, checking to see who is passing through. When they see Billy with his light skin and hair, they call a halt and insist that a levy be paid, not only for him, but also for King George and Ruby. The amount they ask for is far more than the last few remaining coins that King George is carrying. No amount of fierce bargaining on King George's part is winning them over.

Billy remembers all too well how good his dad is at handling situations like this. King George is very good at many things, but diplomacy is not one of his gifts. Billy wonders what he can do to step up and take a leaf out of his dad's book. Unfortunately the party does not have any humbugs, or for that matter any other kinds of sweets, and Billy doubts that the officials will let them through for Snow-White the scrawny chicken. Then he has an idea.

While King George gestures wildly, making his own strange wailing noises, Billy unzips the side pocket on the pack, pulls out three diamonds, and slaps them on the counter.

The reaction is instant. There is complete, awestruck silence from all parties. King George can't believe that Billy is giving away their riches. The customs men think that all their Christmases have come at once! For a moment, their eyes nearly pop out of their heads, but it will not do, to seem too eager, so they try to look nonchalant, and don't make any comment for a few seconds. Then one of them picks the diamonds up, and examines them as if to check they are real and says: "Well this is highly irregular, but I suppose these will just be enough for three of you."

After that, they are all very good friends, and there is much smiling and backslapping as the men lift the gate for the three travellers to go through. Billy is rather pleased with himself. He has succeeded where King George was clearly failing. King George has a dark look on his face, and for the next few miles he mutters and tuts, and won't even look at Billy. Now any bargaining depends on one chicken and a few cans of food.

Ruby starts to recognise her surroundings, an anthill first and then the fields and trees. They are nearly at her village. A week has passed, but there is still the smell of soot and burning in the air. She comes up close beside Billy and takes a firm hold of his hand. Billy in turn, grabs hold of King George by the hand. They go forward together. Ruby is crying softly as the village comes into view. King George is expecting it to be bad, but he is shocked at the total devastation all around him. The fire has even crept into the bush, burning as far as can been seen to the east. Part of the brick chapel stands, but nothing else. None of the bodies have been moved, though some have been mauled by animals, and there is a terrible stench in the air. The travellers each put an arm over their faces to shut out the smell. Ruby pulls her friends in the direction of her mother's grave where she kneels and cries uncontrollably. The little piece of cloth that Ruby left there has not moved. She picks it up and holds it close. Billy and King George stand by quietly. They both sense that it will do her good to cry, but the smell is so bad that after about a minute they lift her gently onto her feet and coax her away. There is not much breeze, but what there is comes from the east, so once the travellers are south of the village, the smell quickly dies away. Ruby is still crying when they reach the cottage.

Billy remembers that he was on his own when he was last here. King George busies himself getting the chicken fed, and making some food for the children. There are still some packets of soup left, and a bottle of Marmite. King George takes the soup for making a stew to which the corned beef will be added. Billy takes the Marmite and jumps across the first two stepping stones across the fast flowing stream that will grow into the mighty Zambezi. The third stone is about four feet long and completely smooth from many years of wet season water flowing over it. Here Billy sits in the evening sunlight, dangling his feet into the crystal clear water, dipping his finger into the Marmite and savouring its delicious salty taste. With the sound of the river he does not hear Ruby as she lightly jumps out to join him. She sits close to him and leans her head on his shoulder. He offers her some Marmite, and she recoils, making a disgusted face. This is the reaction Billy usually gets when he offers to share his Marmite, he even hopes for it.

"Just imagine," he says, splashing his feet, "this water will flow a thousand miles and then drop over the Victoria Falls. I wonder how long it will take, and how many adventures it will have on the way!"

Ruby sighs and says: "Soon you will be with your mum and dad..." They both know that the unsaid ending to her sentence is ..."and I will never see mine again." They sit quietly until the sun drops below the trees and King George issues his own very unique call for them to come in and eat.

Billy wonders why his little cloud seems to be growing again, but then he remembers that he is not very far away from school. He wonders what has happened in the time he has been away. How did everyone react? What kind of a search was made? Where do his parents think he is? Will they really be at Kalene? Billy often spends the last waking minutes of his day talking to God. Tonight he prays for protection, he prays that he will soon be reunited with his parents, and he prays for Ruby; "Please God, you know how sad she is. Please do something to help her." Troubled thoughts gradually give way to sleep.

King George remembers his promise to Billy. He will not take him back to the school, but this leaves him with a problem. The school lies right between the travellers and their destination, and King George is now out of familiar territory, so he indicates to Billy that he will have to show the way. Billy responds to this by drawing a map on the ground showing the route he remembers the school lorry taking on Sunday evenings. This route will take them round the east side of the airstrip, with the school being to the west. Beyond the airstrip the road comes to a farm owned by Billy's uncle. Billy does not really want to come into contact with his uncle while he is on the run, lest he should return him to school, but provided the travellers can get past the farm unnoticed, the road loops round from there and joins on to the Kalene road. From there they will be on their way without any problems.

The walk back to the road leading into the school takes longer than Billy expects, but eventually the tall white sign marking the junction where the road branches off to the school or leads straight on to the farm, comes into sight. By now the sun is low in the sky, and Billy has forgotten what day of the week it is!

Billy sneaks quickly past the junction, anxious to get away from the school as fast as he can. The others follow, and soon they are safely walking down a rarely used track. Then in the distance Billy hears the growl of a truck engine grinding into life. He knows the sound of that lorry!

"Sunday! It must be Sunday! He whispers to Ruby, a look of panic on his face. The lorry will take about five minutes to reach them, and it will be driven by Mr. Birch! The thought terrifies him even more than being chased by 5 Commando.

"This way!" says Billy urgently, as he drags King George into the bush hastily followed by Ruby and the chicken. The trees here are sparse, and there are waist-high shindwa plants all around them, their little red fruit, sticking up brightly above the soil. Billy turns to see the school lorry approaching in clear view along the road. It is full of excited children. Then to his horror, the lorry slows, growling its way through the gears and comes to a stop. Children are jumping off even before the truck has halted. They fan out in small groups and as individuals, hunting for shindwas. There is nowhere better to run to, so the travelers crouch among the vegetation, like sheep hiding in bracken, and hope that Snow-White will not cluck too loudly.

The sound of chattering children is getting closer and closer. Billy's heart is pounding! "Please don't let them find me!", he prays silently. They are so close that Ruby can see the shoes and socks of children running by not more than ten feet away. Then right in front of Billy the shindwa plants part, and he is confronted by his two old friends, Jonnie and Mike!

Disbelief is written all over both boy's faces. Billy looks pale. He raises his fingers to his lips, wide eyed, and then whispers, "Please don't tell anyone, please". The boys can see that he is terrified, and yet they are in two minds as to what they should do.

"Where have you been?" asks Mike quietly.

"Long story!" says Billy. "I'll tell you one day, but not today. I have to get to Kalene". Then the boys see Ruby and King George, still hiding. "They're helping me get back to my mum and dad."

"Mr. Birch will kill us if he ever finds out we saw you here!"

"What do you think he'd do to me!?"

There is a short, awkward pause, then Jonnie says, "OK, we won't tell," Both boys turn just as some other children arrive behind them.

"Come on," says Jonnie, "there are more shindwas this way," and he leads the party back towards the road.

The travellers creep through the undergrowth until they get to a safer distance from the road, and then wait until, with great relief, they hear the lorry's horn calling the children back. Silence is golden.

Near to the farm there is the mission chapel. Billy has noticed, when surveying the inner fitments of the chapel during a particularly boring service, that one of the window latches is broken. He hopes that it has not been fixed.

It is dark by the time they arrive there, and King George has to hold Billy up so that he can push the window. With a little bit of effort, the window finally opens and the travellers scramble inside. They eat baked beans and sausages by candle light and use cushions provided for old ladies as pillows and mattresses. They all sleep well, and no one sees then slip out of the window at dawn for the final leg of their journey.

"After a mile or so, the road forks again. This time one road goes right to the school and the other will take them through Ikalene, not to be confused with their final destination of Kalene. Billy feels apprehensive. "What if they are not there?" he mumbles to himself. "What if we turn up at the mission, and they are not there? The missionaries are sure to take me back to school!" This thought worries Billy more and more as they arrive on the outskirts of Ikalene, and spend their last pennies on three bottles of warm cream soda which they drink, sitting on a concrete wall running along the back of the shop, out of sight. Billy writes this question on the floor for King George to read.

"Ruby can ask someone coming from the mission" King George writes in reply.

So as soon as they are on the road again, they look for someone suitable to ask. A woman with a large enameled bowl on her head comes towards them holding on to a toddler, and followed by another child a bit older. Ruby approaches and talks to the woman whilst Billy, feeling conspicuous as the only white boy around, tries to stay hidden.

Soon she comes trotting back with a smile on her face. "They are staying with the doctor. Your mother is working at the hospital, and your father is teaching. She said that every day they were trying to find their missing boy. Mr. Brown has his plane at Kalene for a week so that an aerial search can take place. He is flying today, so you must be careful.

Billy is so happy he could cry. Instead he gives Ruby a hug that lifts her right off the ground.

Kalene Mission is built at the bottom of a dramatic escarpment, on top of which Billy's great grandparents built the first mission in this part of Africa, not very long after David Livingstone marched through on his famous trek to discover the Victoria Falls. In those early days, before malarial drugs had been developed, it was vital to live away from mosquitoes, and the top of a hill away from standing water was the best place to do this.

Slowly out of the heat haze the blue ridge of the escarpment rises up to the west. Knowing that there is a search going on from the air, King George decides to get off the road and walk on paths through the bush again. This takes them up the back of the escarpment from a small stream, and brings then out on some flat rocks, rippled with the fossilised ridges of an ancient beach. Here there is a dramatic view over the bush to the north, looking back into the Congo. Billy feels that he can see the whole of his adventurous escape from school up here. The travellers sit on the rocks, with aloes pushing up through the ancient cracks.

Billy reaches out his hand to take Ruby's. "I wonder if I would have run away, had I known everything that was going to happen," says Billy thoughtfully.

Ruby smiles. "I'm glad you ran away."

Billy proudly shows Ruby the big rock where his ancestors first settled sixty years ago. There is a plaque there, still screwed to the rock. It reads:

Kalene Hill Mission
Was founded in 1905 by Dr Walter Fisher
Of the Christian Mission in Many Lands
Here were the first hospital,
school and post office of the region

The path leads along the ridge for about a mile and then drops between some large boulders down the steep side of the escarpment. There ahead of them glimpsed through the trees is the mission station. Billy can even see the roof of the hospital way below them. After about two hundred yards the path levels out on a shelf running along the cliff. Here to the left is a shady spot where the vegetation has found plenty of moisture and the grass is green. Billy runs to catch King George's arm.

"What is it?" asks Ruby.

"This is a special place for my family. Look." Billy begins to pull away the grass. Soon the end of a stone grave begins to appear, and after pulling away a bit more undergrowth, there is a headstone. "This is where my great granddad and great granny are buried." King George has heard of Dr. and Mrs. Fisher. Their family is spread out all over this part of Africa now, working in Congo, Zambia and South Africa. He feels a little bit awestruck at finding himself standing by their grave. The inscription features their names, Dr. Walter Fisher, and Susanah Elizabeth, and the dates of their deaths in 1935 and 1938. Billy has been here twice before. Once with his mum and dad, and once with the school. They make regular "pilgrimages" to this spot to honour the founder. But there is another, more precious reason why this place is special to Billy.

"Help me tramp down the grass over here," he says to Ruby. So together they flatten down another area about ten feet away, until Ruby catches her foot on a rock about nine inches across. Billy kneels and pulls away at the grass, to reveal three stones, like small loaves of bread standing side by side. Squatting beside them he looks up at Ruby.

"This is my brother," he says. "He was only four days old when he died, and he was eight years older than me, so I never met him." There is no headstone. In fact there is no way to know that the three little stones mark out a grave, unless you have been told. "Mum and Dad didn't want anything fancy on this grave. They prefer to think of him being in Heaven, not here."

The tiny grave is a poignant reminder of the hardships of early missionary life, and the many children who lost their lives to tropical diseases or just complications in childbirth, complications that would not have been fatal in an English hospital. Billy rests his hand on the middle rock, and sits quietly, then he says: "Bye, bye, little big brother." and gets up to leave.

After twenty minutes of bouncing and clambering down the hillside, the path suddenly flattens out and makes its way between manioc, groundnut, maize and pineapple fields, and then on to the road that they have been avoiding. King George reckons there is no harm in them being seen now. Billy starts to run towards the hospital.

"Wait for us", shouts Ruby excitedly. "I can't run while I'm carrying Snow-White." King George takes charge of the raffia basket. Snow-White has got used to being carried in it, and somehow she has avoided getting eaten right throughout the journey. King George doubts she will survive until tomorrow. Not with the celebration that must be round the corner!

Billy bursts in through the front doors of the hospital and runs down the corridor. A white overall clad orderly scolds him as he literally slides around the first corner and nearly crashes into his mother! She drops the pile of notes she is carrying and then steps back, mouth open and lost for words. Billy does not stop. He throws his arms around his mum, as if he will never let go. She hugs him and begins to cry. "Where have you been?" she says quietly. Billy does not reply. Ruby and then King George come around the corner. Faith's eyes open wide. She is trying to work out how and why he has appeared.

Billy undoes his hug, and takes Ruby by the hand, gently bringing her forward to meet his mum. ""This is Ruby, and she doesn't have a mum and dad any more. Please can she live with us?"

Faith dodges the question but stoops to greet Ruby, who for the first time since Billy has met her looks shy. She shakes hands politely but carries on looking at the floor.

"Hello Ruby," she says kindly, lifting Ruby's chin with her finger so that their eyes meet and then she says to Billy, "Come on, I think we had better go and find your dad. He is teaching some of the patients who are good readers, how they can become teachers in their villages. He is up at the school. The children will all have gone home from lessons now.

Faith slips off her white coat and hangs it up, calling to one of the orderlies to explain her absence, and then the four of them make their way up to the school.

John is just stepping out of the thatched school house. He has had a busy day. He stretches and takes a deep breath of fresh air, preparing to go in to deliver his last teacher training seminar. He takes off his glasses and wipes the sweat from them. As he does so he sees the party coming up the drive towards the school. His eyesight is poor, and he can't see who they are until he puts his glasses on again. Then he gasps. "Billy!" he says. The two run towards each other, like the moment the Prodigal Son comes home. John kneels on the road and Billy envelopes his dad in a huge hug, buries his face in his shirt and cries, until he is sobbing uncontrollably.

Ruby, looks on. Her own eyes fill with tears, and then overflow so that they roll down her cheeks and splash onto the floor. She is so relieved and happy for Billy, and yet this reunion has laid her own loss bare. Soon she is sobbing too, for the loss of her parents. The commotion has not gone unnoticed in the class room. One by one the students come out to see what is going on. They stand about on the decking outside the classroom.

Suddenly Ruby stops crying and looks! Then she shouts; "Papa, my Papa!" She runs past the Walkers and up the steps onto the decking, and throws herself into the arms of a man with a big scar down one side of his face. He is weak and thin, but he is recovering and he cries as he is reunited with his daughter. The other students, unaware of all the details burst out into spontaneous applause.

John abandons his last lecture and sends his students home early. "Come on, let's all go and drink tea, so that we can hear each other's stories." Ruby's dad comes too.

And that, since we have arrived at a well-rounded happy ending, might be that.

But it isn't.

Chapter 29

Billy and Ruby talk over the top of each other as they narrate the events of the last two weeks. John, Faith and Kutela can hardly believe their ears, and there is the shock of finding out about Ruby's village and the death of her mother. A shock almost too much for her dad to take.

"At least I have you," he says to Ruby. "And to think, you were the only one left alive! And I only escaped because of that dog bite, and because the missionaries freed me from the spirit-man's men just as they were about to throw me to the crocodiles!"

John and Faith listen anxiously as Billy describes the plane crash and they hear about Pedro.

"He gave his life to bring you to Mutshatsha," says Faith.

Everyone listens incredulously as Ruby describes how they found the diamonds, and Billy explains with pride how they were used to further their journey. Inside John reflects on how the children have valued freedom higher than material possessions, and how Ruby is a much more precious gem to his son, than even the Blue Butterfly. It makes him wonder whether Billy has any idea how much the diamonds are worth. Such ponderings are academic since all the diamonds have now gone.

All the adults are sure that the children are grossly exaggerating the size of the Blue Butterfly, until King George, who has never been known to lie, confirms it by indicating that it was the same size as the teaspoon in the sugar bowl (minus its handle).

"Goodness!", says Faith, a little wistfully. "A blue diamond, that big! I'm sure even the Queen of England doesn't have one like that! I would like to have seen it, not to keep, you understand, but just to admire!"

Snow-White is sitting in her raffia basket on the floor next to King George. Everyone's thoughts turn towards supper, and the general consensus is that chicken would go down well. Billy has grown attached to Snow-White over the last few days, but he has learned not to be sentimental about food, so he says goodbye to her, and John takes up the bag to do what is necessary. He carries it out to the back of the house accompanied by King George. With him gently holding the chicken, John tips the bag upside-down and turns it inside out.

Snow-white is not the only thing to fall out of the bag, for there on the ground lies a flawless, fifty nine carat, pear shaped, blue diamond.

Appendix 1:

From "African Folk Tales". Singleton Fisher. C1939

BEE AND HONEY-GUIDE.

The purpose of this tale is to explain why Honey-guide leads people to honey. This little bird has a great liking for the larvae of bees. He has discovered that man and the honey-badger are able to break open the hollow trees in which the bees make their honey and has learned to lead them to it. When the bird sees a man passing he flies over to a tree near the path and chatters away fussing about with his wings to draw his attention. If the man pays no attention the bird will follow him for quite a long distance chattering and chirruping and fluttering his wings, going from tree to tree either beside or in front of him. As soon as the man gives a loud whistle indicating his willingness to follow the bird, the honey-guide flies off in the direction of the honey alighting and chattering on trees every forty or fifty yards or so to wait for the man. When he comes to the tree in which the honey is, he is unable to indicate the exact hole into which the bees are flying but he stops chattering and makes a soft whispering note, flying from tree to tree around the one in which is the honey. The note sounds very like "Tala, tala," which in Lunda means "Look, look." When the man has discovered the hole by which the bees enter and has cut open the tree he will take the honey, and a lot of the larvae will fall out of the comb while he does it. Most Lunda and so can afford to wait eat the comb with the more tender larvae. If the man lives nearby, he will often callously set a trap and bait it with larvae to catch the honey-guide as, like the Italians, the Lunda like to eat small birds. We have many times followed a honey-guide

(Retype)

BEE AND HONEY-GUIDE.

and been led to honey *by him*. The Lunda say *that at* the honey-guide can be very spiteful and *can* lead you to a lion or a snake instead of to honey. The Lunda hunters often get very irritated with the bird who persistently follows them and by his chatter warns the game of man's approach. We have many times had a big game hunt spoiled in this same way. The game know that *the* honey-guide does not chatter unless a man or honey-badger is near. The Lunda say that the honey-badger when he hears honey-guide's chatter gives a grunt and is led to the honey in the same way as Man is. The badger's strong claws enable him to break open the often rotting tree and his tough hide is impervious to bee stings.

An account of this was published in The Times, August 24th 1937. The Lunda are very amused when you explain to them that honey-guide leads them to honey to get the young bees and larvae, *and* they reply by telling this tale.

To make a friendship This would begin with a solemn avowal of friendship and an interchange of gifts which as we have mentioned in notes of an earlier tale would be maintained. They were both eating well. This is an idiom implying the happy interchange of gifts mainly of food.

It is a common practice for a child to be sent by the Lunda on messages of this sort. They have wonderful memories and are less liable *they think,* to be bewitched. One is frequently astonished to see the amount of confidence thus put in quite young children. Honey-guide's song was evidently a weeping song. When a Lunda bewails his dead he generally does so in song. He will lock his

BEE AND HONEY-GUIDE.

hands behind his head and if sitting down will lean back against the wall of a hut or against a tree, and wail in a musical chant that has a heart-rending note of sadness about it, mentioning the reasons for the death of his beloved and referring to the happy times they had together. Honey-guide's mourning song is a very limited specimen of what really happens. Most of the Lunda agree that the women are more skilled in weeping than the men. *The women, they say,* have more tenderness in their hearts and greater capacity to express it. I remember sitting for half an hour listening to an elderly Lunda bewailing her dead brother who had been poisoned by his enemies. The language she used was beautiful in the extreme and reminded me of David's death dirge about Solomon and Saul. See 2 Samuel ch.I v.19-27. The expression <u>mother is gone</u> is a quotation from the death dirge sung when a person dies, by the "spirit" men(tudyañu) who wave their rattles over their dead saying "<u>Today he is gone, he is gone</u>"

Appendix 2:

A mercenary fighting for the West in the Congo gives the following account:

It seemed to me we had been taking villages apart, innocent villages of peaceful farming folk who did not want any part of this war, all the way along the track from far down in the south. We would turn up unexpectedly, open fire without warning, race through the place, burning every pathetic shanty and shack to the ground regardless of who might be inside. The idea was to spread the image of our determination and ruthlessness; to terrorise the whole area; to give the rebels an example of what they were in for... It seemed almost certain that the villagers knew nothing about the activities of the rebels...Unsuspecting women were hustling around, carrying water and going about the last of their day's chores. Children were playing in the dust, laughing and shouting to one another. We paused for a few minutes, and then came the order to fire. There was a great crackle of shots from machine guns and our deadly new Belgian rifles. Women screamed and fell. Little children just stood there, dazed, or cartwheeled hideously as bullets slammed into them.
Then, as usual, we raced into the place, still firing as we went. Some of us pitched cans of petrol on to the homes before putting a match to them. Others threw phosphorus hand grenades, which turned human beings into blazing inextinguishable torches of fire. For a while, as we raced along, there was bedlam. Shrieks, moans, shrill cries for mercy. And, above all, the throaty, half-crazed bellowing of those commandoes among us who quite obviously utterly loved this sort of thing. Then, as we moved away beyond the village, the comparative silence, the distant, hardly distinguishable cries of the wounded, the acrid smell of burning flesh. These mercenaries were trained to never, 'in any circumstances', take prisoners: Even if men, women and children come running to you... even if they fall on their knees before you, begging for mercy, don't hesitate. Just shoot to kill.

A Revolutionary Life, John Lee Anderson. P610

Wikipedia: Congo Crisis

Printed in Great Britain
by Amazon.co.uk, Ltd.,
Marston Gate.